A WINTER PROPOSAL

AUSTIN RYAN

 *To Amanda,*

for our beautiful friendship, and to spite

every poisoned memory from our pasts.

And to Kieran,

whose kindness, strength, and courage is

 *on every page of this book.*

Your softness is your strength.

PRONUNCIATION GUIDE

Cian = KEE-en (Irish for ancient or enduring)
Saoirse = SEER-sha (Irish Gaelic for freedom)
Ask = AHSK (from Old Norse for ash tree)
Ingerid = ING-rid (from Old Norse for Ing is beautiful)
Kari = KAHR-ee (Norwegian short form of Katarina)
Johannes = Yo-HAN-es (Norwegian short form of John)
Erkki = EHRK-kee (Finnish form of Eric)
Liisa = LEE-sah (Finnish short form of Elisabet)

CHAPTER 1

THE NORTHWOODS, TWENTY DAYS BEFORE
THE WINTER SOLSTICE

I once was a girl who believed in magic.

Faeries and trolls were as real to me as the dancing colors in the night skies above our cabin. The stories my grandmother told by the glowing hearth fueled my imagination until I saw traces of magic everywhere. I saw faerie folk dancing in the sparkle of drifting snow, felt their power in my grandmother's soothing touch, their irreverence in the brook's laugh through the ice. But when the woman who loved me like a daughter died, my childish beliefs had done nothing to save me from the cruelty that followed.

Sitting on the frozen stone steps, the chill seeps through my wool skirts, pressing the cold winter day into my skin. I pull my shawl tighter around my shoulders.

Across from me and down the road, scattered log cabins are draped in winter darkness. Snow blankets the slanted roofs and stone slab steps in the little town I've called home for just a quarter of my life.

Muddy sleigh tracks and hoof marks sparkle with frost, and the shiny layers of ice catch the flickering glow from torches held aloft by housefolk moving quietly between outbuildings.

It's been almost a decade since my grandmother died now. And still, her presence feels no further away than the stars winking down at me from the velvety darkness above. The quiet of early morning stretches around me, even if it looks like night —we're too far north for the sun to rise for hours yet.

My grandmother's laughing voice sounds in my ear, flavored by the lilt from her island roots. "For our endless summer nights, we pay a steep price in winter, Saoirse."

She wasn't wrong. Most days, the little daylight I see is through the windows of the Pedersen's main house, while I scrub floors and empty night pots. If I'm lucky I'll catch a bit of sunset when extra hands are needed for the afternoon milking.

A creak erupts in the stillness, pulling me out of my thoughts. A tabby cat pushes through my neighbor's half-shut door and slinks away down the path between our two cabins.

I shiver as the memories of my grandmother inevitably morph into the memories of after she died. Faded images of my life with the aunt who took me in flash through my mind, twisting their blades painfully in my chest.

I shoot up from the steps and stomp into the alley as if memories like these can be outrun. But if there's a chance—I'll give it my all.

Silver-frosted grass crunches under my boots as I follow the tabby down the alley between the two cabins. I'm desperate to escape both the ache in my chest and the prying eyes of my neighbors. Will the solitude in the hollow of naked, frostbitten trees down the hill from our cabin be enough? It will have to be.

The dark-striped tabby is merely a shadow as it pounces on thin air, streaks across icicle grass, and is swallowed by the snow-laden vines.

My boots scrape the frozen ground just like the grief does my raw heart. My grandmother's stories shimmer and clatter in the cold air the same way her laughter once did between the buildings.

The darkness pooling in the shadows makes my imagination run wild.

Soon, I'm eleven again, seated at her knee by our hearthfire as her stories fill the air, twisting and curling like the sharp smoke tickling my nose. Her warm hand rests on my shoulder as she tells me of *Huldra*, the beautiful cow-tailed faerie woman luring young men down into the mountain—never to be seen again.

Her eyes hold mine as she warns me:

Never trust the faeries, Saoirse, they know no other way than deceit.

Gooseflesh prickles down my spine as I remember her story of the farmer who refused to pay the faerie taking care of his animals, only for it to kill off all the farmer's livestock. Another about a faerie dancing a servant girl to death for stealing the promised lump of butter from his porridge.

Don't try to bargain with the magic folk.

Other stories spin through my mind, no more flattering of the faeries than the ones before. But for all her warnings, I'd still believed the magic folk was more than evil faeries. Surely those faeries who danced in the ribbons of light in the night skies would save my grandmother when she fell ill? Didn't faeries know the secrets of life and death? Didn't they have healing magic?

For weeks I kept my eyes peeled for striking tree stumps or a darkened hollow, ready to strike whatever bargain needed to heal her.

But the faeries never came.

And when I was sent to an aunt I'd never met, I waited with bated breath for the magic folk to find me. Surely they were just delayed?

Their magic would save me from the bruising force of her anger, wouldn't it?

I'd run away from my aunt the first chance I'd gotten, long

after I'd realized that the faeries would never come. Because they didn't exist. My grandmother's stories had been just that —stories.

And while lights still dance in the skies over my home, there is no magic in it. The sparkles in drifting snow are just the reflection of sunlight. The laughing brook only trapped water. And my grandmother's love died with her.

Blood seeps freshly from a wound over ten years old, and I press my hand against my heart as if I can still the flow from the outside. But there's no use.

I wipe away the moisture on my cold cheeks as the cat crawls ghostlike out from the brambles. Did it catch its prey already?

I crouch down to call it when a flash of bright light stings my eyes, and my voice freezes in my throat.

When I blink my eyes open, the cat is gone.

In its place is a man whose snow-white shirt sleeves are a sharp contrast to his dark waistcoat and the breeches tucked into tall boots.

The air in my lungs turns to ice as I try to comprehend what my eyes are telling me. He can't possibly be what I think he is, can he? Faeries were ugly in my grandmother's stories, repulsive to the humans who crossed their paths. Only when they wanted a human's favor did they possess ethereal beauty—like the cow-tailed woman or the faeries who swapped human children for their ugly changelings.

But this man, with his sharp jaw and high cheekbones, smooth, golden skin, and full lips? Ethereal is the only way to describe this man.

No human could look this perfect.

And no human could transform from a cat to a man in a flash of light, Saoirse!

My mouth goes dry as I spot the most damning evidence of all—certain those are pointed ears sticking out of his hair.

I hold my breath as each and every childhood story swirls inside my head until bile tickles the back of my throat.

Faeries don't exist. They are stories, Saoirse. Folklore, faerie tales, fiction.

But while I was once happy to embellish my grandmother's stories, to let the faeries be kind to humans, I know those were only the fantasies of an innocent child. If faeries *are* real, they must be like my grandmother told me—unpredictable and conniving, without regard for human life.

I shudder soundlessly in the dark, not daring to move a muscle.

The man sighs deeply and removes a dagger from the leather sheath at his waist.

No.

Not the man. *The faerie.*

The blade in his hand, sharp-edged and deadly, catches the faint light from the snow, and my stomach sinks further. I have nowhere to hide in this barren winter landscape, and the eerie half-light in this hollow will be no match for a faerie's sharp vision. If he turns even slightly, he'll see me.

Fear holds breath captive in my chest.

A faerie would think nothing of killing a human, and I have just seen this one shift from a cat to a man. What will he do once he realizes I know his secret?

My heart thrashes against my ribcage, thundering so loudly he *must* hear it.

I need to run, to at least try to escape. But as much as my legs ache to get me out of here, what is the use? The faerie will only halt me in my tracks with a flick of his wrist.

I close my eyes, and ragged breaths saw in and out of my lungs as I wait for him to see me. To kill me.

Time drags on as I wait for the end, but nothing happens.

When I finally open my eyes, the man, faerie—whatever he was—is gone.

CHAPTER 2

I run from the hollow to the cabin, legs moving faster than they have in my life. Terror nips at my heels, claws at my heart, seeps into my bones. With every booming heartbeat, hands pull at my skirts, my hair. Strong, tanned hands wielding a sharp blade, ready to take my life away from me.

My heart and lungs are close to bursting when I finally cross the threshold, into the warmth and light from the hearth. I slam the door shut on the silvery winter night outside, and sink to the floor.

Ingerid's dark skirts swirl around her bare ankles as she jumps away from the simmering pot in the hearth. Her hand slaps to her chest. "You startled me!"

But then she gets a better look at me propped up against the door jamb, gasping for breath, and she frowns. "Are you all right, Saoirse?"

I try to answer, but my teeth chatter too much. How do you tell someone you've seen a faerie?

It takes several deep breaths before I gain control over my voice, and even then, I stumble over my words. "I saw a tabby cat, but it wasn't… I mean, it looked like a faerie, and I thought. I closed my eyes and—"

Ingerid tosses her honey-blonde braid back over her shoulder, and sighs. "Do you think maybe you fell asleep out there?"

Did I?

"Yes… I think I must have." Relief trickles through me as I clamp onto the explanation with a desperation fit to the terror still pounding through my veins. The three of us stayed up too late last night—I must have dozed off on the steps, that's all.

It was a nightmare. Only a nightmare.

Of course there wasn't a faerie in the hollow, Saoirse. You were thinking of how much you missed your grandmother, and then you dreamed about her faerie stories.

It's been so long since her death, but I don't think I'll ever be rid of the ache. Especially not on these dark winter mornings that remind me of her.

"It sounds like it was a rough one. How about I warm some honey milk for you?" Ingerid pushes the porridge pot to the side of the hearth, already reaching for the smaller pot hanging from the hooks above the fire.

I nod, and my hand barely shakes as I pull out the bench tucked under the table where three wooden bowls sit ready for breakfast.

At twenty-two, Ingerid is barely a year older than me. None of us have ever known our parents, but it's never stopped Ingerid from taking on the task of mothering Liisa and me. I never would have made it through my first night alone in the Northwoods if she hadn't shared her hiding place with me, nor would Liisa, if we hadn't found her that same night.

I gulp down the honey milk and let its warmth spread beneath my breastbone and into my veins. Slowly, it banishes the terror in my bones. By the time Liisa stumbles into the room, looking more dead than alive, I feel almost like myself again.

My youngest found sister staggers to the table—her thick, dark hair still a mess from sleep. "I need to go to the smithy—" Her words are cut off by a yawn and the scraping sound as she pulls out her end of the bench and dumps herself onto it. She rubs her eyes as if she's much younger than her twenty years.

"The blacksmith?" Ingerid turns a sly gaze on me as she joins us at the table, flicking her braid out of reach of her porridge bowl. "Why don't you have Saoirse run your errand? She needs to go there, too."

This is news to me. "I do?"

Ingerid's grin is bright in the flickering light, and mirth dances in her eyes. "Yes, you do." She almost sings the words, but I'm still confused.

Across the table, Liisa shoves a spoonful of porridge into her mouth as if it can stop her next yawn. It doesn't, but when the yawn lets go of her, she nods to me. "You can go for me, Saoirse, but what are you doing there?"

"I'm… not sure?" I look to Ingerid for an explanation.

Her eyes widen, then she huffs. "Not something. *Someone*, Saoirse."

My cheeks heat as I catch her meaning.

Liisa and I serve at the Pedersen farm for the use of this old cabin, and Ingerid's long days at Erkki's father's farm keep us in food. But when the blacksmith's son shaved off those awful sideburns at the end of last winter, I realized what I should have long ago—that three orphaned girls can't live on their own forever.

We'll have to marry and find homes of our own sooner rather than later. And Ask, especially sans sideburns, is a fine choice for a husband.

Ingerid smirks, pausing her spoon halfway to her mouth as she reaches for the red butter dish. "He won't ask you to be his wife if he never sees you, will he?"

"I guess not?" I pull in a deep breath, and the excitement

tingling in my chest melds with the comfort of the honey milk. Just for a moment, the warmth and safety of my grandmother's hearth feels within reach again. *A real home.*

"He won't." She plops a pat of butter onto her porridge, and the yellow lump is like a warning bell. Ask's lopsided smile fades in my mind's eye, and the terror of this morning floods my veins. Would the faerie I saw in the hollow kill for a stolen butter lump?

Faeries don't exist, Saoirse, remember? You don't believe in magic.

I close my eyes and steady my breaths, trying to calm my thundering heart. But it's no use, because no matter what I told Ingerid, and tried to tell myself, I know what I saw.

And as I later strap on my wooden skis to trek through the winter darkness for another day of endless scrubbing of clothes and floors at the Pedersen farm, my grandmother's stories swirl in my head.

They never scared me as a child. Armed with the love that always surrounded me, the cruel behavior of the faeries was no worry of mine. But as I recall the stories now, each one is more terrifying than the one before.

Not because I'm no longer a child—but because they are no longer stories.

CHAPTER 3

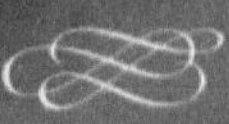

S pruce trees, tall and heavy with snow, stand sentinel along the path as I ski home through the woods. Changelings' pained cries carry on the wind, and a tendril of fear snakes through my chest. Soon, a hulking troll looms in my periphery, and I whip my head around, catching my breath as the terror rattles my heart.

But no, it's not a troll, just the same snowladen boulder I pass every night.

I stop and stab my long ski pole into a snow bank. With my hands free, I tighten the shawl around my shoulders. Then I pick my pole back up, put my grandmother's stories out of my head, and hasten my speed.

But the memories of the magic I saw as a child won't leave me alone. Not now that I've admitted to myself that my faerie sighting wasn't a nightmare.

Because if the magic folk were real all this time, why didn't they save me?

I was a child—I deserved to be saved.

But I already know why, even as her voice echoes once again. *Because the faeries cannot be trusted, child.*

Minutes later, I unstrap my skis, and lean them up against the side of the cabin. I knock my boots against the steps, and—as the caked-on snow falls off—open the door.

I've had no more encounters with magical beings in the two days since I saw the faerie in the hollow. Unless I count the shiny eyes flashing from my neighbor's stone steps as I returned that night. The memory of the cat's unnerving attention has goosebumps spreading across my shoulders even now. Thankfully, it's nowhere to be seen as I lift the latch and go inside. I pull off my shawl, hood, and mittens, and rub my arms for warmth.

The mending basket filled with red and blue stockings sits ready for me on the table, and my sigh is a plume of white smoke in front of my face. After preparing a cup of steaming coffee, I sit down and pull the first of Liisa's stockings into my lap. An hour later, the basket seems as bottomless as when I started.

A barrage of filthy words, loud enough to penetrate the thick window glass, pulls me out of my thoughts. A horse whinnies wildly, and a child cries.

Drawn by the ache in my chest at that last sound, I push open the door. The frame groans as if what I'm about to see won't be to my liking.

And it isn't.

Resting my cheek against the cold door post, I try to make sense of the scene in front of me.

The brightly painted sleigh stopped on the road screams of its owner's wealth. As does the driver in his heavy fur coat, poisoning the air with profanities directed at the crowd by the side of the road. But a sleigh this fine is not a common sight in this small Northwoods town, and I don't blame them for staring.

The driver's whip whistles through the air as he takes his rage out on the team of onyx horses. One of them rears up. Ears flat against its head, its powerful hooves cut through the air before it returns to the ground with a thundering sound. A little girl squeals and presses into her mother's dark skirts.

The cries that first pulled me out here, turn to a wail, and I search for the source.

My neighbor, a handsome man if not for the angry grimace twisting his features, has one meaty fist hooked into his little boy's collar as he hauls him away from the edge of the street.

Big tears stream down the child's red face. "I didn't run into the road!"

The man's snarls are too low to hear over the still cursing sleigh driver and the chatter of the crowd, but the boy winces. Still he wrenches free from the man's grip and fists his small hands on his hips. "I need to get my cat, you don't understand! He saved me from getting hit!"

"If I see that cat again, I'll kill it myself, do you hear me?" He tosses a glance in the direction of the stomping horses. "It's as good as dead already."

Another sob from the boy twists my stomach. He throws a last look towards the street where the driver is still trying to control the horses, and the heartache etched on his face is too much. His pleading eyes catch mine, and I can't look away.

"Please, my cat." His words aren't directed at the sorry excuse of a man pushing him towards the tarred cabin next to mine. They are directed at me.

Cold settles in my stomach as I move out of the doorway, jump off the stone steps, and sprint towards the road. I make my way through the small crowd until my nostrils fill with the filthy stench seeping through the ice broken by the stomping hooves.

I blink and strain my neck to catch a glimpse of the boy's cat. There, under the sleigh is a dark shape in the slushy mixture of snow and mud. Its striped fur is darkened with blood, but I'm certain it's the boy's cat.

Except, it isn't truly that.

Fear swirls in my stomach as terror dances through my memories of that morning in the hollow. Surely it's the same creature that shifted into a faerie? What good could possibly come from saving it?

"Better just end its miserable life!" From the side of the road, my irate neighbor shouts the words I can't deny are in my own heart.

The boy howls, a door slams, and they're gone.

Compassion stirs in my heart, but can I truly save the life of this creature, knowing what it is? But what if the boy was right and this faerie saved him from being run over?

Faeries don't save children, Saoirse. You know that better than anyone.

And I do.

After all, I have the scars to prove it.

The sleigh inches forward with a loud groan, the runners about to cross right over the animal's spine. Not pausing to think, I throw myself forward. "Please stop, sir! You'll kill it!"

But heedless of my cries, the sleigh shudders away over the uneven road with a sickening crunch. The driver's ugly curses are too faint to penetrate the haze in my brain as bile rises in my throat. I clamp my hand over my mouth, certain I'll hurl at the sight about to meet me. Dipping my head, I search the muddle of snow where the sleigh passed and glimpse lumps of bloodied fur. I shudder, and look away.

But while I might not mourn the life of an evil faerie, the little boy's pleading eyes won't let me leave the animal he loved out here to be tossed about like trash. *Faerie or not.*

I kneel in the frozen mud, bracing for the touch of lifeless flesh. The metallic scent of blood fills my nostrils, and I hold my breath. Pressing my hand against the icy ground, I scoop the feline up, cradling it gently. Its body is still warm, and fresh blood soaks the dark sleeves of my jacket. And then...

It moves.

Not a spasm, but real movement.

It's alive.

I gasp as fear wars with hope inside me—I'm holding a living faerie in my arms!

Thundering hooves and swishing runners sound again, and I barely manage to jump out of the way as another sleigh rushes past me.

Scandalized whispers reach my ears. "What is she doing with the dead cat? It doesn't belong to her, does it?" A woman I don't know leans forward to glare at me.

"Look at the state of her dress!" Kari Bakken clutches her little sister's hand as she sweeps a glare of disdain over my soiled clothes.

I roll my eyes. A little boy was almost hit by a sleigh and they care about the state of my clothes? But my problems are bigger than that right now. I need to get the faerie, cat, whatever it is, inside—away from the prying eyes of the crowd before it shifts. Can it still shift?

The shivering body stirs in my arms, and I quicken my steps, careful to avoid the icy patches.

My neighbors tip their heads together, and their whispers are like a buzz on the air. All eyes are on my stained dress and the bloodied lump in my arms. But the only set of eyes I care about are those in the tearstained face pressed against the thick window glass of the cabin next to mine.

Finally, I push my door open, letting out a breath of relief as it creaks shut behind me. One-handed, I spread a clean linen towel on the table.

Liisa doesn't often return before dark, and Ingerid won't be home until after dinner. The sun rose not long ago, so there are several hours left of daylight. Can I tend to the cat and return it to the boy before either of the girls come home?

But as I look at the barely breathing creature in my arms, I know there's no way—it's too badly injured. I lower the cat onto the table, remove my filthy jacket, and unbutton my wrists to shove my now stained shirt sleeves to my elbows.

The crunching sound of the runners sliding over the animal's back plays on repeat in my mind, and a violent shudder shakes my shoulders.

Its spine *must* be broken—it shouldn't have survived the heavy sleigh, and yet, its warm belly rises and falls under my hands. Because of its magic?

But couldn't a magical faerie have evaded the sleigh in the first place?

I try not to think of what I'm really doing as I cleanse the deep lacerations across the cat's back. The water in the basin turns more pink for each swirl of my cloth. I wring it out, again and again, until I'm certain the wounds are as clean as I can get them.

Keeping an eye on the table, I rifle through a chest for Ingerid's healing salve. I pull the waxed fabric off the pot, and breathe in the scent of sunshine and honey, thankful for a reprieve from my nasty task. Dabbing the sticky salve at the broken skin along the cat's back, I tie another linen strip around it. Then I repeat the process along its silky underside.

One more swipe of my finger through the velvety contents of the tin, and I spread it across the last scrape. The striped fur grows warm, then smooths under my fingers. I hold my breath as its color darkens and the markings fade.

The sudden appearance of smooth, golden skin is the only warning I get as the air cracks and a flash of lighting blinds me.

A limb is shoved into my stomach.

A string of dark curses fill the room. And then, I'm staring into frosty green eyes.

Faeries aren't real.

The faerie's gaze drops, and I follow it to where my hands

are clutching his warm waist. His *bare* waist, save for the strips of bandages.

Heat rushes to my cheeks as I pull my hands off his skin and back away from his knee. His bottom half—*thank God!*—is covered by the dark cloth of his breeches.

"No need to move your hands on my account." Even slurred, his melodious voice tugs at something behind my ribs, flooding my body with heat. His smirk is more than suggestive, and I open my mouth to retort when another crack sounds.

I shield my eyes from the sharp flash about to follow.

But there's no light, only more curses, and when I drop my hand, the faerie is on the floor—the broken pieces of our table sticking out from under him.

Fear chills my stomach as he pushes to his feet and his hazy eyes meet mine. He sways, and another weak curse escapes him as his face grows even paler. Then his eyes roll back in his head, and he crumples into the broken table.

The crack of the surface slab splinters the air, and I wince, but the faerie doesn't stir.

I stand frozen as bright daylight streams into the room from the window by the door, illuminating the unbelievable scene in front of me. A half-naked, wounded faerie on top of our broken table.

I pull in a weak breath, and settle trembling fists on my hips.

I might need to amend my own belief in magical beings, and question why I thought they'd come for me. But if my grandmother's tales are true, I can't expose my sisters to this danger. What if Ingerid comes home early?

I'll need to find a way to hide him away until I can decide what to do—except, how on earth does one hide a faerie? Especially one so large?

He needs to wake up.

I tap his leg with the toe of my boot.

His build might be lithe compared to Ask's, but he's still both taller and wider than me, and I won't be able to move him on my own.

I bend to give his warm shoulder a shove. "Wake up!"

He whimpers, but his eyes stay closed. Strips of linen cover the worst of his wounds and I've applied the sticky honey-salve to the rest of them, but he's still mostly naked. And there's no way I can move him without touching him.

I groan.

Move him? Where on earth will I move him? I have no chance of getting him upstairs, but where else is there?

I yell at him a few more times, but I don't dare touch him again.

Pulling my wide sleeves to my wrists, leaving as little skin exposed as possible, I bend and wrap my arms around his torso. His shoulders jam up under my chin, and his clean-shaven face is much too close to mine. Dark blonde hair brushes my temple, and my skin pebbles. His skin is smooth and warm under my hands, against my cheek. *No it isn't. He's a faerie!*

Droplets of sweat trickle down my back as I pull him off the broken table pieces and across the threshold to the rough hewn slabs of wood leading upstairs.

He groans, and startled by the sound, I almost drop him. As I resettle my grip, his eyes are still closed, his body still dead weight in my arms. I don't let my gaze linger on the smooth muscles of his stupid abdomen. *Faerie, not ogling material.*

The stairs to the second floor have never been so steep, or so long. I make it up two steps before I need a break. I hope faeries don't bruise easily, because I have no way of preventing the backs of his calves from hitting every single step as I haul him upwards.

Halfway up, my hands are slick with sweat, and I lose my grip. He slides down my body until his face is no longer next to mine, but halfway down my torso.

He moans and turns his face, practically smashing it into my heaving chest. "Ey, how did I get here? I like this."

Oh God, I'm going to combust from embarrassment.

He makes no move to stand, and I refasten my grip around the upper part of his torso, pulling him away from my chest.

"Where are you taking me, my heart?"

He did *not* just call me that. But though his words are slurred and he can't know who he's talking to, my heart gives a little jolt at the endearment. A jolt I immediately shut down. "I can't have you passed out on our broken table."

"Am I your... scandalous... little secret?" There's no mistaking the flirtatious tone this time.

I ignore him, groaning as I heft him up another step, and suddenly his face is so close to mine. Too close. His eyelashes flutter against my cheek. "Oh, I like this even more."

"Well, you're the only one. I don't like this at all." I grind out the words, cursing whoever first decided second floors were needed.

The faerie's lips brush my jaw, and I can't tell if it's an accident or not.

Of course it's an accident, Saoirse.

"You don't like me?" His breath is warm against my neck. "I'm pretty sure you're supposed to like me." His voice is pouty, like that of a little boy not getting his way.

I roll my eyes. "And *I'm* pretty sure you need to lay off the butter on your porridge. You're—" I grunt as I heave him up one more step. "Too heavy."

He tsks. "Maybe you need to get a bit stronger, little human."

An answer is on the tip of my tongue, but then he goes limp in my arms. Again. When I get a look at his face, his eyes are closed and his lips parted.

I wish I was the one passed out, rather than the one needing to pull a full-grown man the rest of the way to my room. If faeries had to be real, couldn't they at least have been a little lighter?

CHAPTER 4

Liisa dances through the doorway, a dark silhouette against the yellow evening sky. Her cheeks are rosy with cold, and her dark eyes full of laughter as she brushes the snow out of her hair. "Erkki's friend needs better aim. He wouldn't hit a moose at four paces."

I raise an eyebrow from my seat on the bench. "If that's the case why is your hair full of snow?"

She shrugs and untangles the snowy scarf from around her shoulders. "He hit the tree next to me, and it splattered." Droplets of melted snow fly through the air as she flings the garment over a hook on the wall. Then she stops dead. "Saoirse, what in the sprucewoods did you do to that table?"

I've had hours to clean up rags and salves from caring for the faerie's wounds, but there's no cleaning up the pile of broken boards that used to be our table. "I… uh, fell on it."

"You fell on it?" Liisa's face is a mask of disbelief. How much wider would her eyes go if she knew the mess of planks is the work of the faerie hidden away in my room?

A real faerie. Wonder battles with terror in my heart. My

grandmother's stories *were* true—the magical folk I believed in as a child are as real as I am.

And they didn't come for me.

And they're likely every bit as evil as she claimed.

The magic folk know no other way than deceit. The warning rings through my mind, and the terror wins out again.

Liisa shrugs out of her jacket and spreads it over the chest in the corner, where it drips melted snow onto the planks below. Her frown deepens as her gaze trails down my body. "It just doesn't seem like you'd be quite heavy enough to reduce our table to that." She waves her hand in the direction of the broken remains.

No, Liisa, it was actually crushed twice by the weight of the faerie that is now in my bed, and he's much heavier than he looks. I rub my sore arms, but I'll really feel the strain of pulling him upstairs tomorrow.

She glances at me again. "The waist of your dress is a bit large, do you want me to size it down for you?"

I look down at my tightly laced waist. There used to be plenty of room for my snow white shirt to peek through between the two sides. Will Ask care that there isn't now?

The thought makes me want to slap myself.

How can I worry about the fit of my dress when there's a wicked faerie upstairs in my room? A seriously injured wicked faerie. What will he do when he wakes up? How can I make him leave before the girls realize he's here? And what of his terrifying moral code? Will what might annoy a human justify murder in a faerie's eyes?

And you shoved, and kicked, and dragged this one up the stairs.

I'm going to be sick. Tears clog my throat, and words slip over my lips before I can stop them. "Liisa, I don't know what to do." I hate the despair in my voice.

But Liisa only wraps her arms around me, rocking me back and forth as if I'm a child in need of soothing. Her clothes are still cold from skiing home, but as she presses against me, my chest expands for the first time since I brought the cat inside. Whatever mess I've found myself in, I'm not alone.

"Don't cry, Saoirse. We'll find a new table, and your dress waist looks fine the way it is. It's not worth crying over." Her voice is soft against my ear, and I nod, even though she doesn't know the half of it. Then she swipes a tear off my cheek and dazzles me with her smile. "Why don't you slice some potatoes, and we'll fry it up with the leftover moose meat? Ingerid won't be back till after supper, so it's just me and you." *And... the faerie in my bed.*

Nausea twirls behind my red waist, and I don't think I'll be able to eat at all.

I EAT ENOUGH to stave off Liisa's worried glances, and return to the bottomless basket of stockings. Long after the darkness has settled, Ingerid finally returns home.

She shuts the door behind her, leans back against it and lets out a deep sigh. Her teeth tug at her lip, and the happy glow on her face would rival even the midday sun.

I exchange a glance with Liisa.

Ingerid is often in a good mood when she returns from her days spinning and weaving at the farm across town where the farmer's handsome son finds any excuse to get her alone. But this seems different.

When she pulls off her frozen scarf and yellow and blue mittens, her cheeks are red from more than the cold. The smile on her lips can't be wiped off even by the sight of the broken mess between the benches. "Erkki asked me to be his wife."

Liisa gasps, jumps up, the half-darned stocking dropping from her hands to the floor as she does. "What? When?"

Ingerid's eyes are shiny, and I know what this means to her. Erkki's father could easily do better for his son than an orphaned girl, no matter how pretty or kind. And Ingerid is both. She's cried on my shoulder, more than once, for fear that Erkki would be forced to marry a girl closer to his own social standing.

Ingerid lets out a breath of laughter, eyes full of light and hope. "He asked just now. He says his father doesn't care as long as he stays to work the farm with his brother."

But, of course, that's not enough to still Liisa's curiosity, and she tugs Ingerid over to the bench closest to the hearth and pushes her down. The fire crackles cheerily as Liisa flops down on a goat pelt on the floor. Then she gasps, and a frown takes over her face. "You don't even have a chest ready—we need to sew!"

She counts on her fingers the sheets, blankets, and clothing that Ingerid will need. She'll have no dowry, but we'll find a way to make sure she brings *something* to this marriage.

Ingerid's laughter is full of hope and girlish dreams, but when I try to join her, my own catches in my chest. How can I laugh when there's an evil faerie waiting for me upstairs? One that could snuff out the happiness around me without even trying?

Faeries cannot be trusted—they seek mischief always.

The words dig their claws into my bones, and I hate that I can still feel the warmth of the faerie's smooth skin under my hands. I rub my palms against my coarse wool skirt, hoping it will wipe the sensation away. Handsome or not, he's a faerie, and I'd be a fool to think his face is one of virtue.

"Did you kiss him?"

My face heats, and I let out a squeak of protest. But Liisa's question is of course directed at Ingerid. Liisa gives me a funny look. "Are you... are you all right, Saoirse?"

My blush deepens as I nod, eyes glued to my hands. "I'm fine, just tired."

The faerie is already messing with me, and he isn't even here!

Liisa shrugs and moves her attention to Ingerid who's also blushing, though for a different reason, I suspect. "I did… and I can't—" She drops her grinning face into her hands and squeals through her fingers.

Liisa yawns, but waves her hand for Ingerid to go on. "I want to hear about this kiss before I go to bed."

Liisa's dark eyes glitter as Ingerid turns even redder. But then she tells the story again and again, until every bit of pleasure has been wrung out by Liisa's *oohs* and *ahs*.

But I can't concentrate on Ingerid's words. Not knowing what awaits me upstairs.

"Liisa!" Ingerid's laugh draws my attention.

Liisa blinks awake, straightening. "What?"

Ingerid throws a ball of mustard yellow yarn at her. "You just fell asleep mid-sentence!"

Liisa wipes a line of drool off her chin. "I did not!" But her eyes blink shut again a minute later, and she's not hard to convince to go to bed.

I stay with Ingerid, trying and failing to follow her story. She's too full of dreamy sighs to notice my lack of attention. Still, it's almost midnight by the time I make it upstairs to my own room.

I pause outside my door, the iron latch cold under my fingers. But nothing will change if I wait another hour. *Unless he's already gone?*

Surely a closed door wouldn't keep a faerie put if he wanted to leave? I step over the threshold and hastily shut the door behind me.

The room is dark, but outlined against the faint light from the snow outside, is the man on my bed—*the faerie.*

CHAPTER 5

"That's a deep sigh for a human. Anything I can help you with?" His voice is scratchy, but still smooth enough to make my heart beat just a little faster.

Foolish heart.

I press my back against the cold door and try to swallow my fear, but it sticks in my throat, not slowing my rapid heart at all. "I need to go to bed."

The bedding rustles, and I hear the smirk in his voice as clearly as if I could see it. "Well then, don't let me stop you. There's plenty of room here."

That's the furthest thing from the truth. My bed barely fits me, and wrangling a faerie at least a head taller than me onto it made that very clear.

But then, in the dark, he says the last words I expect. "I need your help."

I draw in a quick breath. "What?"

The bed creaks, and he lets out a pained grunt. "I need you to go check on Finn."

"Finn?" The name comes out a croak, but I don't know anyone named Finn.

He huffs, as if my confusion is pretense. "The human boy next door."

The father and son next door keep to themselves, so I've never heard the boy's name spoken. Has their cat been a faerie all the time we've been neighbors? Unease crawls in my chest, and my gaze flits to the pitch-black winter darkness beyond the window pane. "I can't go check on anyone right now. It's the middle of the night."

He moves as if to sit up, but falls back with a groan. "His nights are the hardest, it's why I stay there." He curses under his breath, but I can't get past his last sentence.

"You shift into a cat to look after a human boy?" My confusion makes me forget for a moment that I shouldn't make conversation with the faerie. "Why?"

Quiet sinks over the room. Clearly he's not going to answer that. He moves again, and his breath hitches on another curse. The crunch of sleigh runners across his back sound again in my memory, and my heart aches at his pained grunt.

I take a step closer. "Are you in pain?"

"No. But I can't..." He groans. "I can't shift." The intensity of his gaze is a living thing in the dark as the bed creaks under his movements. "Which is why I need you to go check on him."

Is he for real? How does he think humans operate? I fist my hands at my hips. "I can't go knock on their door in the middle of the night. I'm not a cat, and I can't shift into one either."

"I can fix that for you. I think you'd enjoy the process."

Is that humor in his voice?

His gaze trails down my body as if he's touching me with his hands, not his gaze.

Do faeries see better in the dark than humans do? I fold my arms over my chest just in case. "If it involves magic, I absolutely will not."

He smirks, and I ignore the way it makes my stomach tumble.

Pinning him with another glare I ask the question that's been nagging at me since he shifted into a human earlier. "How did you even get run over by a sleigh in the first place? Aren't faeries supposed to be more aware than that?"

I sense more than see his eye roll. He clears his throat. "I was distracted."

"By what?" What would distract his otherworldly senses to this extent?

A quiet grunt fills the air, and I suspect he lied about the pain. "My charge next door running in front of it?"

His *charge?* Did he really save the child, then? But why?

He sighs, but makes no attempt to explain. The strawbed rustles again, then his voice again. "Will you go tomorrow?"

"What is his father doing to him that requires you to check on him?"

"His uncle. And he's doing what any pitiful human does when life doesn't go his way—abuse those weaker than him with words and fists."

Memories flood my mind, pulling me out of this dark room and into another. *One smaller and darker. Where terror sinks its claws into my body while I cry against the locked door. In a world where I'm helpless, yet again. So much smaller, weaker, than my aunt's fury.*

Sadness stirs in my gut as I remember the boy's tearstained face. Then scorching anger tightens my muscles until they ache.

I may not be strong enough to give my neighbor a taste of the terror he dishes out to his nephew, but I'm no longer the helpless child I was. "I'll go in the morning."

The faerie opens his mouth as if to protest, but I cut him off. "He'll be asleep now anyhow."

His dark, humorless chuckle fills the air, and a shiver trails my spine. Does he think the boy is not asleep? My own sleepless nights at my aunt's house sweep over me—*the cool pillow against my tearless eyes, the aching loneliness burrowing into my bones.*

But even if Finn isn't asleep, I can't go over to his house at this hour. Even tomorrow, I'm not sure exactly what my presence would do.

The bed creaks again, pulling me out of my dark memories. "You better come to bed then, so you'll wake up in time."

Come to bed.

I shiver. There isn't room in the bed for both of us—not to sleep.

My heart jolts into a faster beat as unbidden images crowd my mind. Being pressed up against the firm chest that emerged under my fingers earlier. His hot breath against my cheek, his lips against my jaw. Like on the stairs.

His arms... I tremble, and not from revulsion. *No! Faerie. Danger.*

"I'm not going to sleep in your bed."

"But you want to?" His voice is dark and syrupy and it melts against my skin. And it's exactly why faeries shouldn't exist, and why I should stay away from them if they do.

I ignore his comment, as well as the heat in my cheeks, and move on to the more pressing question. Where *will* I sleep?

My room is much cooler than the downstairs where I've spent the last few hours. But Ingerid is already asleep on the bench by the hearth, and if she catches me stretched out of a goat pelt in the morning, she'll only have questions I can't answer. Or worse, decide to investigate my room and find the faerie.

No, I can't put her in danger like that. I'm only letting him stay until he's well enough to go back where he came from, and the less my sisters know, the better.

That leaves the chilly floorboards in my room as the only option. With a last longing glance at my soft bed, and *not* the half-naked man reclining on it, I sink to the floor.

I curl up, and try to ignore the quiet breathing of the faerie in my bed.

And the presence of magic in my world.

CHAPTER 6

My hips and neck are screaming, and my backside is completely numb. How did I ever fall asleep in such a horrible position?

I wince and push away from the unyielding planks of my bedroom floor.

"There would have been room in the bed, you know."

I hold back my screech at the last second and stare at the man lounged against the headboard of my bed—his broad, bruised chest still on display.

I press a hand to my heart, and will the wild panic there to subside. How could I have forgotten *why* I was on the floor?

Forest green eyes dance with mirth as he takes me in. That cad is enjoying my reaction! But then the smirk falls from his features, and his face grows serious. "Will you go check on the human boy now?"

I gape, my voice rusty with sleep. "Now? It's barely morning."

From his steely gaze, he disagrees.

"Alright, alright, I'll go as soon as I can." I groan and attempt to stretch my aching spine. Moving to the door, I push it open just a crack. But the hallway is clear, and soon, I move stiffly down the stairs. Every downward step is followed by a shooting pain in my hip, and when I finally arrive downstairs, it's to the clatter of wooden bowls and Liisa's soft curse.

Ingerid is leaned up against the hearth, fully dressed and with her porridge half eaten already. She smiles wide when she sees me. "Saints! I forgot to tell you!"

She's bubblier than should be allowed at this hour. But although she's being forced to eat her morning porridge standing up, at least Ingerid slept in an actual bed, not crouched up on the floor.

I groan and rub my sore hip. "Forgot to tell me what?"

The glint in her eyes tells me I'll enjoy her news, too. "Erkki said he thinks Ask likes you, and that he always brings you up when they talk."

A smile pulls at my lips then, as tired and groggy as I feel, because how can it not? My heart swells in my chest, because Ask might just help his father now, but one day he'll be the blacksmith. And I know him well enough to know he'll use his strength only to protect, never to harm me. In short, he's everything I've ever wanted in a husband.

Everything I've ever wanted from life.

In my mind, Ask's earnest eyes gaze deeply into mine as he asks me to be his wife. His large hands, calloused from years of smithing wraps around mine. But before I can succumb to my daydream, his eyes turn the color of pine forests, and the hands wrapped around mine are ones with strong, slender fingers.

My smile drops, and I push that particular face out of my mind. Faeries are evil. And even if this one is hot as blazes, it doesn't change what he is—*dangerous.*

UNDER THE LIGHT of a new moon and armed with half a honey cake wrapped in a scrap of linen, I cross the alley between our two cabins and knock on the door.

Last night's snowfall has erased the path down to the hollow, but I still glance towards the trees with unease in my stomach. The faerie I left wounded in my room might not be there this morning, but are there others?

I turn my attention back to my task and rap my knuckles against the wood again. All is quiet inside, and it's so early I don't dare call out. After the third series of knocks, soft footsteps close in on the other side of the wall.

The door opens a crack, and flickers of lamplight mingle with the dark around me. A boy no more than ten-years-old peeks out. His green eyes are guarded, but then they flare with recognition. "My cat! You have my cat! Is he well?"

My heart bleeds at the desperation in his voice. "He's hurt, but he'll be just fine. I'll take care of him until he's well enough to stay with you again."

"Is he hurting?" The boy's eyes shine with unshed tears, and I hesitate.

I don't want to lie, but the worry in his eyes slay me. "Not so much anymore, I think."

The boy swallows and looks down at his bare toes, before he quickly wipes his face. "Will he be better tomorrow?"

I'm opening my mouth to answer when a sharp voice rings out from inside the cabin. Finn's flinch is like a sucker punch to my gut. He looks over his shoulder, as still and trembling as a hare that's just sensed a fox. *And I feel his reaction in my bones.*

"I have to go." He shuts the door quietly, before I have a chance to give him the honey cake. Angry shouts penetrate the timbered walls, and I want nothing more than to take Finn with me. Far away from here, far away from this pitiful excuse of a human in charge of him.

I stand frozen in the dark as the urge to storm inside tears at me like a gale. I don't know how much time has passed when I finally force my feet to move across the snow and back up the steps to my own cabin.

The honey cake thumps against the top of a chest just a second before my elbows slam down beside it. I sink to the floor, and my fingers close over my cold face.

I don't want to remember.

It's been six years since I ran away from my aunt's house, and still I can't shake her presence. Her slicing words chisel away at my self worth, now as they did then. They still reverberate through my skull—whispering, gloating—when I close my eyes at the end of a long day.

Running away might have saved me from further abuse, but all of me didn't make it. Parts of the girl I was are still at that house, and I can't have them back.

I can never have them back.

A hand lands on my shoulder, and I swallow a scream as I whirl on… "Ingerid? I thought you left to see Erkki?"

Her eyes widen as she takes in my face and drops her hand from my shoulder as if my wool sleeve might burn her. "I just got home, what's the matter?"

I shrug the old wounds away. I haven't told Ingerid that part of my story—neither about the bruises I hid nor the sharp words that chipped my soul. But Ingerid has never needed to know the wound to offer healing, and her gray eyes soften. "What do you need?"

I shake my head.

I don't even know how my heart can still crack and bleed over cuts that happened years ago—how would I know what is needed to fix them?

Ingerid looks around the room before her eyes still on the coals in the hearth. "A cup of coffee? A hug?"

I try for a smile. "Both of those will do."

Her eyes crinkle at the corners, and she wraps me in a hug

far more solid than her spindly arms should be capable of. But Ingerid hugs me with her heart, not just her body, and it makes all the difference.

It takes three cups of coffee to still the gaping hole in my stomach. By the time I sip the last of the bitter brew, Ingerid has left again, and I have no further excuse to delay my trip upstairs. Where I'll need to talk to the faerie.

Stalling for time, I grab the jar of salve from yesterday and some more rags. I should have checked his wounds last night. They were frightfully deep when he was in cat form. Are they as deep in his current form?

I ascend the steps with slow movements and tap my fingers on my bedroom door in warning.

His words attack me before I'm fully into the room. "How is Finn?"

I shoot him a glare he absolutely ignores. "You're not supposed to be here. Will you please keep it down?" We might be the only ones at home right now, but there's no way to know for how long.

He repeats his question, erasing the effect of all three cups of coffee. His eyes search my face, and he curses, eyes wide as he jolts to a seated position. "Is he hurt? I swear humans are disgusting creatures."

I can't disagree with him, but I shake my head. "No. I don't think he's hurt. Not yet. His…" What had he said the man was? "His uncle was yelling at him."

A snort comes from the bed. "That's the least of it." He watches me intently for another moment. "If the boy is fine, why do you look so unsettled?"

I press my lips together. "I don't look unsettled."

"No?" His accent that I can't quite place is so strong on that one word, and it's clear he doesn't believe me.

The back of my eyes burn, and I drop my gaze to the space under the bed. Dust bunnies look guiltily back at me. I really need to sweep in here. I can go to the woods and fashion a new broom later today. Except that I really don't want to give myself any additional reasons to spend time in this room. With him.

When there's no longer a risk of tears, I turn my attention back to the faerie. "Finn seemed very worried about you."

Softness slips into his gaze, and his features relax in the light reflecting off the snow outside. "What did you tell him?"

"Just that you were hurt and would be back with him soon."

His throat bobs. "Good."

I step closer to him, and his gaze slips down to my lips. Lingers there.

My stomach makes an odd tumble. Pretending as if that's normal, I raise the rolled-up linen strips so he can see them. "I need to check your wounds."

He shakes his head. "They'll heal on their own. I have magic, remember?"

I snort. As if I could forget. "But they were so deep, and I thought your magic wasn't working right? You said you couldn't shift?" My gaze skims over his broad chest. The bruises do seem more faded than when I first woke up. Or maybe my night of terrible sleep has just rendered me less observant?

He moves as if to get up, then pulls air through his teeth.

The sound makes me flinch, and my eyes flit to his face—but there's no anger on his features, only pain.

He pushes out another ragged breath. "That's because *shifting* requires a lot of magic, and healing my wounds takes precedence."

I let my full hands drop and step back. "If you're sure."

His head dips, and he leans back onto the pillows. Perspiration coats his pale forehead, and despite my misgivings, compassion stirs in my heart. He's obviously still in a great deal of pain, but none of his words today have been about his own injuries, only concern for the boy.

But how can that be?

A memory from one of my first weeks with my aunt seeps into my mind like a fog between trees in the woods. I'd spent night after night awake, scouring the moonlit woods for any sign of a magical being coming to save me. But the woods had stayed empty.

It hadn't taken me long to conclude that if the faeries did exist, they must be every bit as evil and uncaring as the stories had claimed. And I've kept that belief.

But if they are so wholly evil—why does this one care so much about the welfare of a human child?

CHAPTER 7

Our little log cabin is filled with cheer and warmth that night. Flickering tallow candles toss a golden glow over the wooden bowls topped up with Ingerid's fragrant moose stew and cups filled with mulled wine. Both of my sisters kneel on goat pelts while they eat, and Liisa's contagious laughter fills the air.

But it's all wasted on me.

No matter how safe I am now, I can't get Finn's pale face out of my head. Can't shake his wince at his uncle's voice or the shadows under his eyes. No amount of crackling flames in the hearth seems able to dim my own memories, or the idea that Finn is as good as living them next door.

That helpless terror sits in my bones still, so many years after the bruises faded. What good is my own escape if there's nothing I can do to save this little boy from the same fate?

My heart is heavy as I trudge up the stairs after supper, shutting myself into the half-dark of my room.

"What's wrong?" The faerie's voice startles me, and I turn to see his frown dip between his brows. "You look unsettled again."

I let out a weak snort. "Why do *you* care?" My voice cracks on the last word, and I blink my eyes furiously to stop the tears burning behind my eyes. I can't look at him. Not when he knows how affected I am. My gaze trails the uneven floorboards instead, the ones that still need a good sweeping.

When he doesn't say anything more, I glance over to where he's propped against the pillows at the head of the bed.

His eyes are narrowed, his voice quiet when he speaks. "You really think me a monster, don't you?"

I move to the chest at the end of the bed and fumble to light the lamp. As soon as the flame bursts to life, the golden glow pushes the shadows to the corners of the room.

"What gave it away?" I glance back at him over my shoulder.

His eyes glitter at me from the bed, where he looks oh so comfortable. "Your fear."

I adjust the wick and straighten. "Faeries can see fear?"

He huffs and rubs a hand down his too-handsome face. "We have eyes—the way your shoulders hunch and you shrink away when I speak isn't invisible."

I straighten. "Why do you care that I think you're..." I swallow the words about to roll off my tongue. "...that I don't like you?"

Insulting an evil, unforgiving faerie? Not your best idea, Saoirse.

My teeth sink into my bottom lip.

His gaze moves to my mouth, and his eyes darken. It's there and gone so quickly I might have imagined it. Did I?

He clears his throat, and if there was any heat in his gaze before, it's gone now. "I care because out of the two of us, yours is the breed that fosters monsters."

My eyes narrow. "No, it isn't."

Does he even know what he is? Does he know the stories humans tell about his kind? That my grandmother told?

"Is Finn's uncle not a human?" His voice is quiet, but too controlled—as if it's all he can do to rein in his anger. But his anger at what?

I shudder and wrap my arms around myself. "Presumably."

"And whoever hurt you was as well?"

Color drains from my face, and my stomach turns to ice. "What?"

The word is breathless, frozen on the air. What could he possibly know about my life at my aunt's house?

He shrugs his broad shoulders, drawing my attention to the shadowy bruises that still mottle the skin down to his collarbone. "We don't have to talk about it. But you came back from Finn's looking like you'd seen a ghost, and you still do."

I try to swallow, but there's something stuck in my throat. My eyes burn again, and I bend over to pull on my boot laces. Why can't I loosen the hold of my memories as easily?

"Are you still going to insist on sleeping on the floor?" I feel his eyes on me as he speaks.

I kick my boots off and consider the spot where I slept last night. The chill of the floorboards already bites into my stockinged feet. And the hip I slept on last night is as sore and bruised as my heart.

I don't think I can make it through another night like that, but to sleep in the same bed as a faerie?

I turn back to him, certain this is my worst idea yet. "Will you keep to your side?"

The air simmers with tension when he answers. "Like a gentleman."

Which I'm fairly certain he isn't, but I'm too heartsick to fight tonight. I just want sleep. One full night where I'm not visited by the nightmares I left behind all those years ago.

Heart pounding, I walk around the bed. The straw mattress rustles as he scoots over, leaving enough room for a small child. Since that doesn't begin to describe me, I'll definitely sleep good and pressed up against him. But does it matter?

I reach for the woven blanket, but as my fingers curl around the edge, I freeze. "Wait. I don't know your name."

He rolls his eyes, a puff of laughter on the air. "If that's what it takes to get you into my bed."

My grip tightens as I narrow my eyes at his stupidly handsome face. "It's *my* bed, not yours."

"Cian." The word floats off his tongue and lingers in the air —sweet and magical. Ethereal.

Certain it's part of a language I don't know, I frown. "What?"

"*My name* is Cian."

"Oh." Heat brushes up my jaw. Why does even his name have to be attractive?

His eyes sparkle, and he pats the bed next to him as if there's more than one place for me to lie down. "And yours is?"

I swallow down an emotion I can't name. Desire? Want? Surely it's nothing but the magical attraction faeries command? "It's Saoirse."

He repeats my name, and in his smooth accent it sounds more than beautiful. Ethereal even. My grandmother's stories speak their warnings, but I don't listen. Instead, I climb into bed with a handsomer than should be allowed faerie, and pull the covers over the both of us.

The bed creaks and straw rustles as I try to find a better position. Even pressed against the mattress edge to avoid touching him, it's infinitely more comfortable than the floor. I push my cheek into my downy pillow—it is so soft I want to cry.

And then I almost do. I let out a whimper, and the mattress dips and rustles as my bedmate turns towards me.

He lifts up on one elbow. "What?"

"The light! I didn't blow out the light." This day has been too long already. I groan, and begin to build up the courage to move again.

"Shh. Don't fret, little human, I've got it." The faerie's soothing voice curls inside my chest like warm honey. I shouldn't like it anywhere near as much as I do.

"But you can't move from—"

In the next moment, the room is dark, and for a moment, terror keeps me frozen. "Did you just use…?"

"Magic? Yes. Sleep now, little human. Saoirse." He speaks my name so softly it's like a caress against my senses. And as his melodic voice fills my mind, I fall into a deep sleep.

Without nightmares.

MY BEDROOM DOOR CREAKS, and warm light pushes against my eyelids. Against the darkness holding me captive. But I'm not ready to wake up yet. Not from the best sleep I've had in ages. With a moan, I snuggle deeper into the warm embrace of my blanket.

The creak grows louder as the door is pushed open, and Liisa's gasp echoes off the walls. "What in the world is this? What is that man doing here?"

My eyes shoot open, and as I take in the golden lamplight, several facts strike me at once.

My blankets aren't what's so nice and warm. I'm curled into the faerie's naked chest. And Liisa is standing in the doorway, gawking at me.

I scramble out of bed so fast my knee slams into the cold floor. Pain stabs through my kneecap, and I swallow a whimper as I jump back up, clutching my knee. I'm already blushing from the smirk I'm certain is on the faerie's face. And then more at the thought of having to explain to my sisters why there's a stranger in my bed.

Why did I cave and sleep in his bed? *My* bed.

Ingerid peeks over Liisa's shoulder, face glowing in the lamplight and eyes as wide as I've ever seen them. How late is it that they're both fully dressed? "Saoirse? Why is there… a man in your bed?"

He's not a man!

But I follow her gaze to the bed where the bane of my existence is propped up on his elbows, sculpted chest on full display and a big grin on his face.

How could I let this happen? If I hadn't slept so deeply, I'd have been downstairs before Ingerid and Liisa would have had a chance to worry. And now, I've all but introduced them to a wicked faerie.

As my heart crumbles, he turns to the girls gaping at him from the doorway. "I'm Cian, nice to finally meet the other ladies of the house."

I growl at him. "It's not *finally*. And it's not *nice*."

The girls turn to me with matching raised eyebrows. Liisa props her hands on her hips. "I don't even… I thought you… what about Ask?"

I swallow, and my face burns hotter despite the chill in the room. "This isn't that." I press my lips together over that last word, because there's no way I can explain what it *is*. I rub my sore kneecap and try again. "It's just…. He was hurt. See the bandages?"

I point to Cian's ribs. But the angry red scrapes that once lined the linen strips are already gone, and what was blackened bruises less than a day ago is now mere shadows. There's no visible evidence of how serious his injuries really were— nothing to show what a miracle it is that he's even alive. And I can't tell them without revealing what he really is. Which I can't do without putting them in more danger than I already have.

"So instead of asking for help to nurse him, you decided to hide him in your bedroom?" Liisa looks at me like I've gone mad.

She's not wrong.

"He could have slept on the downstairs, Saoirse, and I could have bunked with you." Ingerid's gaze flits from me to the grinning faerie.

That would certainly have been more appropriate.

I chew on my lip, pressing the words back down my throat. I can't tell them what he is—I need to keep them safe, in any way I can. "I didn't want to worry you."

"I think I'm more worried now, honestly." Ingerid sends me a look that makes it clear I'll have much to explain later. Then she turns her compassionate gaze on Cian. Who doesn't deserve it in the slightest. "Are you hungry? Has she fed you at all?"

I gape, because I haven't. Why hasn't he asked for food?

Cian's cheekbones darken suspiciously, but he dips his head. "Thank you, Mistress Ingerid, I'll have some food, if you don't mind."

I move towards the door to shut it. "I'll meet you downstairs."

With a last concerned look at Cian, Ingerid turns and hurries down the stairs.

Liisa follows her, but with a pointed look at me. "It's almost time for you to leave, Saoirse."

She disappears down the stairwell, and I close the door as panic brews in my stomach.

I make quick work of lighting the lamp. Mistress Pedersen will absolutely chew me out if I'm late, which I will be soon. Saints, it's a good thing I'm already dressed. "I need to leave."

"And it sounds like I have a meal waiting for me." Cian yawns and stretches, putting his broad chest and muscled arms on full display.

Faerie. His looks don't matter.

The reminder of what he is twists my heart painfully in my chest, and I can't help the fear that lingers at the edges of my mind. Ingerid and Liisa don't need to leave until sunrise. Am I really about to leave my sisters alone with a faerie?

I look at Cian, hoping against hope that I'm not making a terrible mistake. "Please don't hurt them."

Cian looks at me as if *I'm* the monster, not he. "Why would I *hurt* your sisters?"

I pull in a shallow breath. "You're a faerie, why *wouldn't* you?"

His eyes narrow, and fear slithers up my back. "You just slept the whole night next to me, didn't you? Without nightmares."

I gasp. How does he know that? "Was that because of you?"

He snorts, and his gaze is cold. "Couldn't possibly have been. I'm a monster, remember? Why would I use my magic to keep your sleep dreamless?"

Words stick in my throat. My dreams torment me worse on days when I'm reminded of my time under my aunt's roof. Is Cian really the reason the nightmares didn't come? But how else would he know? "I'm sorry. Thank you."

He scoffs. "Save it." When he sits up there's no wince.

I swallow down my worry about the change in his mood. "Are your wounds healed?" Completely? They cannot be, can they?

He grunts. "Well enough."

A flash blinds me, and in the next moment, the dark-striped tabby slinks out my door.

I close my eyes and battle the terror pounding in my veins. The tales from my childhood weren't wrong about faeries' temperamental nature—but is that the only truth they hold? And if they were right about the vindictive nature of the magic folk, is it safe for me to leave the girls behind?

I pull in a deep breath, and let it out slowly. Despite my dreamless sleep, sharing my bed with a faerie was as much a mistake as letting Liisa and Ingerid find me there. I need to make this right.

Somehow, I'll find a way to keep them safe.

CHAPTER 8

The tan horse tied to the post by the Pedersen main house snorts and shakes its head, sending the snow in its black and white mane flying.

I can't help but walk close enough to slide my mitten off to feel it's hot, damp breath against my bare skin. Slipping my hand along its muscular neck, I dig my fingers into the warmth under its mane. Leaning close, I breathe in the musky fragrance that reminds me of summer days at my grandmother's.

A head the size of my torso pushes against me. I take several steps backwards in the snow to stay on my feet while a laugh bubbles over my lips. While the horse's head rests heavy on my shoulder, I scratch the soft fur under his forelock, and its heavy sigh fills the air.

Just for a moment, I'm able to forget the events of the last few days. The faerie in the hollow. The cracking sound of his spine under the sleigh runners. Finn's pale face, and his flinch at the sharp voice from inside. Liisa's wide eyes as she found me snuggled into Cian's chest.

All of it a little more distant, a little easier to carry.

I should hurry home, just to make certain the disgruntled

faerie I left behind this morning kept his word not to hurt my sisters.

Fear tingles in my stomach at that thought, just as the horse pushes out another heavy breath of air. But Cian didn't hurt me last night, did he? In fact, I haven't seen him do anything to hurt anyone.

I think back through my grandmother's faerie tales. The magic folk weren't all bad in the stories I heard—they took good care of the livestock, and the horses especially. In some stories they'd punish farmers who didn't care well enough for their animals.

I could get behind that.

"Saoirse!" The shout startles me out of my thoughts, and I search the dark night. A large silhouette emerges in the flickering torchlight. But apart from it being a man's voice, the dark, wind, and layers of clothing obscures everything else. Sliding towards me on wooden skis could be any man in town—Erkki, Ask, or any of their friends.

I'm not afraid, so I stand still and let him approach me. Whoever it is steps closer and pulls the scarf away from his chin. The torchlight falls across the planes of his tanned face. Dark brows over equally dark eyes, and beautifully missing sideburns. "Ask! What are you doing here?"

His broad cheeks darken. "I was… looking for you."

An excited thrill sings in my stomach. Ask was looking for me. Ask who is strong, and steady, and safe. The kind of man I want to fall in love with. Whether it happens before or after our wedding doesn't matter to me.

I give my horse companion one last pat on his shoulder and laugh at his disgruntled snort as I turn my full attention on Ask.

He returns my smile, and waits patiently as I strap on my skis and step sideways to the snowbank where I jabbed my ski pole earlier.

It's so cold I can barely feel my face when we start moving

towards the hill where I live. The steady slide of skis through snow and the jab of our poles every few feet are loud in the quiet evening. At every snow-blanketed cabin we pass, thick window panes throw golden squares of dappled light against the snow. It's that time of day when most people are either already sitting at their tables, or on their way home to do so. "Don't you have to be home for supper?"

Ask's chuckle is deep and husky, the kind that ought to send pleasure dancing over my skin. He tugs his scarf down. "Not many to miss me at home. It's not like I have a wife waiting for me."

I draw in a quick breath, and my voice is barely audible over the snow splattered wind. "Do you... do you want a wife?"

He slows his speed. Our free mittened hands brush, but he doesn't take mine. Is that a bad sign? I hold my breath and wait for him to speak.

"Yeah. Someday, I do." Ask's deep voice is muffled through the scarf he's pulled back over the lower part of his face.

I let out the breath trapped under all my own woolen layers. "That's good." He wants a wife. Now to convince him I'm the wife he wants.

Ask clears his throat. "I heard rumors there's a party down at the tavern to celebrate Erkki and Ingerid."

I perk up. "I hadn't heard that."

Snow whirls through the air, and Ask sends me a sidelong glance, dark and searching. "Maybe you could save me a dance?"

Warmth spreads in my chest. It's happening! "Of course."

He grins, and I send him what I hope is a demure smile in return. We're at the bottom of the hill that leads to my cabin now, but Ask still needs to trek across town to the smithy. Within another circle of snowy torchlight, I turn to face him fully. "Thank you for making the road home short. It feels long some nights."

"I didn't mind." His eyes are so intent on mine that for a

moment, I think he'll kiss me, but then he reaches for my mittened hand and squeezes it. "I'll see you at that party."

I nod, too excited to speak.

My skis slip through the snow as I slide the rest of the way home with a spring in my movements. When I glimpse the warm glow from the tiny windows in our cabin, I move even faster.

Up close the cabin seems bursting with life. Music floats through the bubbled green window pane, broken only by Ingerid's cheers and Liisa's loud laugh. Did Erkki's friend bring his fiddle over?

I cross the lawn as a squeal sounds and boots stomp across the floor. The cheers grow louder as I make quick work of the bindings and prop both skis and pole against the wall. I sprint up the stone steps to join in on the fun, my grin wide as I push the door open.

But the scene in front of me wipes the smile right off my face.

Cian is dancing with Liisa—his strong fingers splayed on her waist with his other hand clasped around hers. Liisa's face glows with happiness, her free hand clutching his shoulder. Dark skirts billow around my sister's legs as the faerie moves her expertly around the floor.

Twirls her around and around—faster and faster.

Until they move over the uneven floorboards at a dizzying speed. Just like the faerie in the story my grandmother used to tell. The one where the girl drops dead as soon as the dance stops.

My stomach turns to ice.

Cian's eyes shine with inhuman intensity, and his wide grin is almost maniacal. How can they not see what he is?

Fear pulses through my bones in beat with the music. "Please stop." I try to shout, but my voice is only a whisper. "Please, Cian."

But he only spins the girl I promised to protect that night so long ago faster and faster, a devilish grin on his face. Bile coats the back of my throat. This can't be happening.

"Saoirse, what's wrong?" Across the room, Ingerid's eyes are full of concern, only Liisa and Cian are oblivious in their race towards death. Or are they?

I pull in another breath. "STOP! I NEED YOU TO STOP!" I bellow the words, and Liisa staggers to a halt, both of Cian's hands on her waist, stilling her movements. "You'll kill her!"

"What are you on about?" Cian's brow wrinkles with confusion, and he lets go of Liisa's hand. I brace, but nothing happens.

Liisa doesn't crumple to the floor. The color doesn't drain from her face, and her eyes aren't wide and staring. She looks very much alive as she folds her arms over her chest and steps away from Cian.

Relief barrels through me, and my shoulders slump. I gulp in a breath of air, suddenly self-conscious with three sets of eyes on me. Ingerid and Liisa stare at me like I might have lost it, more so than this morning, and Cian only looks irritated.

Because I stopped him from killing my friend?

"It was just a dance, Saoirse." Liisa exchanges a worried look with Ingerid, then turns back to me. "I thought you were interested in Ask?"

My throat dry from my shout, my voice sounds like a croak. "I am."

"So why are you worried that I'm dancing with Cian?"

Oh God, she thinks I'm jealous. "Liisa, I'm not… I mean, I like Ask, but Cian is… He's…" Dangerous. But I can't say it. Not while the faerie in question is staring me down with thunder in his eyes—making me feel smaller than an ant.

I clear my throat. "I thought… I thought he was involved with someone."

Understanding dawns on Liisa's pale face, and her cheeks turn pink. "It was just a dance." She looks at her boots, thin arms folded so tightly in front of her chest I worry they'll snap.

"Right." I swallow the words I want to say, ones that will make no sense when I can't tell her the real reason she was in danger. The way she shrinks in on herself makes my eyes burn. I hate that I've hurt her.

"I can't believe you." Cian shakes his head, jaw set and eyes dark as they sweep over me. But more than angry, he seems… hurt?

He stomps out the door and it slams behind him. The music disappears with Cian as the window panes rattle in his wake. All the life is gone from the cabin. Even the fire in the hearth seems dimmer than before my outburst. Was that all from his magic?

I turn back to where Liisa still studies the tips of her boots. The air is charged with distrust, and I don't know how to make it less so. When Ingerid breaks the silence, her words are laced with unspoken reproach. "Is there something you need to tell us, Saoirse?"

I shake my head.

But there's something I need to tell myself. That Cian is a faerie, and that I need to stay far away from both him and his magic. Letting the girls discover Cian was a mistake, one that might cost them dearly if I can't find a way to fix it.

When I have no answer, Ingerid continues with her hands fisted on her hips, which isn't like her at all. "How come we've never even heard of Cian until the moment he's in your bed, where he's apparently stayed for a few days? Where did he come from? Is he a Traveller? Is that why you were hiding him?"

Oh, if only he was one of the many people traveling between towns and villages in the Northwoods, selling goods and services. While they might be looked down upon by village dwellers, they at least are human.

My temples ache. "You didn't ask him?" What did he tell them? Or did he use his magic to avoid their questions?

Ingerid frowns. "He showed up an hour ago, full of apologies about the pressing matter that made him miss breakfast this morning."

I want to roll my eyes. His pressing matter was nothing but a tantrum because I wouldn't trust him. And why would I?

But Ingerid isn't done. "He said the two of you met when you helped him after he got struck by a sleigh. But, Saoirse, I haven't heard of anyone struck by a sleigh for ages, and if he was, why on earth wouldn't you just have nursed him out in the open?"

I have no answer for that, not one I can speak aloud, at least, because *he wasn't a man when he was injured.* And once he transformed into one, all I could think about was keeping him away from her and Liisa.

Worry tugs at her brow when I don't answer. "Where were you tonight, anyways, shouldn't you have been home a while ago?"

The tightness in my chest eases a bit. "Ask walked me home, and..." I swallow, hoping my next tidbit is enough to distract Ingerid from her other questions. "He asked me to meet him tomorrow." Ask, who is the furthest thing from magic there is, thank God.

"Saoirse!" Ingerid's eyes widen, and her brow loses some of its consternation.

Liisa isn't so easy to please. Her gaze moves from the floor to my face as her dark eyes snap with fire. "So the man you want makes a move, and that gives you an excuse to break up my dance with one you *don't* want?"

I recoil from her sharp words. "It's not like that, Liisa."

Her eyes shine with unshed tears. "And if both you and Cian are with other people, why were you in bed together this morning?"

Ingerid gasps. I know Liisa is hurt, I know she's lashing out, and still her cruel words pierce me. The tips of my ears burn as her accusation digs into my bones. "How can you say that?"

But what else would she think? Ingerid probably thinks the same—she's just too good to say it. And even if they believed nothing happened it wouldn't make the two of us sharing a bed any less scandalous.

My shoulders slump as I look at Liisa. "Cian isn't safe! I didn't want him to hurt you, that is all."

Liisa shakes her head. "I can't believe you. You'd think stringing *one* man along was enough, even for you!"

"What do you mean *even for me?*"

But she offers me only a scathing look as she stomps off, much like Cian did minutes earlier. My heart aches as I watch her dark skirts swish around the corner to the stairwell. The slap of her boots against the steps are loud in the quiet cabin, and a moment later, the door to her room slams.

The noise tears at me, and suddenly I'm exhausted. Liisa is safe now, Cian didn't hurt her, and his dance didn't kill her. But that doesn't change the fact that it could have.

Just the thought is enough to send a fresh chill down my spine. But though the dance didn't hurt anyone, the caustic words exchanged tonight still slice at my heart. Will we recover?

Ingerid and Liisa are the closest thing to family I have. My sisters as much as if we were blood, and the possibility that I might lose them, to a stupid fight like this, makes my insides ache. Why didn't I just leave the cat to die? How could I put my sisters in danger like this?

Ingerid says a curt goodnight, and I walk up the darkened stairs with a heavy heart. I can't be certain, but I think I hear Liisa crying in her room.

My heart lurches, and tears well in my eyes. This is what magic does—creates discord. And I brought it into our home.

CHAPTER 9

Sharing this cabin at the edge of town is a far better fate than three orphaned girls should expect. Working as housefolk at the Pedersen farm in exchange for the use of it is more than a bargain.

But though I've slept in this bed since the day we moved in, when the straw was flat and musty under threadbare sheets, this is the first time it has felt empty. I push the ridiculous notion aside as I shrug into my dress waist and old black skirt. As I wrap the worn apron around my waist, I look outside—just in time to see a dark-striped tabby slink out through Finn's door.

I need to talk to Cian. Need to convince him to stay away from Liisa and Ingerid. If he hurts them…. No. I pull in a shallow breath and steady my thundering heart. I can't afford to lose my sisters.

I take the stairs in two steps, wave to a wide-eyed Ingerid, and push down the hurt at Liisa's silence.

I sprint down to the hollow behind the cabin, dark skirts billowing over the white ground. Errant snow packs into the tops of my boots and melts through my stockings, and the air is so frigid my breath catches in my lungs. But I can't worry about any of that now.

I halt my wild run when the tabby jumps out from the frozen brambles.

I'm not too late!

The light flashes. But as soon as Cian is a man again, he loses his dinner in the brambles. The sounds he makes are magnified in the moonlight, and I cover my ears to keep from throwing up myself. I keep my eyes on the snow laden pine tree to my right, studying the ice encrusted needles at the edge of the branch. But I can't block out the sounds completely, and my stomach twists in time with them.

When Cian straightens in my peripheral, I drop my hands from my ears and move closer. "Are you sick?" Can faeries even get sick, or is that only a human trait?

He wipes his mouth with a snow white shirt sleeve as he gazes at me with an unreadable expression. His hair is mussed and shadows line his eyes, and still he takes my breath away. *Because he's a faerie, Saoirse. It has nothing to do with attraction.*

I swallow and wet my dry lips. His eyes glint in the faint light reflecting off the snow, and for a moment his gaze homes in on my mouth.

My heart thunders. Is he going to…?

"It's the shifting." His intense gaze is back on mine.

I clear my throat to find my voice, pushing down the fluttering in my stomach. "Turning yourself into a cat makes you sick?"

He scoffs. "No, little human, turning myself into a cat does nothing. *Staying* a cat for that many hours away from Faerie would make any of us sick."

I frown, trying to understand what he's saying, but I can't. "Then why do you do it?"

His eyes narrow, and he looks every bit the evil faerie he is.

A tremble of fear snakes through me. Seeking him out like this was a bad idea.

"Would it make you happier if I let Finn deal with his uncle's rages on his own?"

I blanch. "No! Why would you say that?"

The faerie shrugs, as if his thunderous expression doesn't make it clear he feels anything but nonchalant about this. "Most humans I've dealt with don't seem to think it a great atrocity to use their fists on their children."

The shadows of each cut and bruise my aunt left digs into my skin, and grief moves through my body. I know that atrocity in my bones. "Clearly you've only dealt with monsters."

He tilts his head, surprise in his eyes. "And yet you're unhappy that I stay here to protect him?"

"Only because you're a—" I clamp my lips shut. Do I have a death wish? The pre-dawn chill digs through my linen shirt until gooseflesh covers my arms.

His eyes turn stormy. "Finish your sentence, human."

I shake my head with jerky movements, as if I'm a wooden doll, not a girl. Darkness swirls in the mossy depths of his eyes, equal parts fascinating and terrifying. He takes a step towards me, and the fear takes over. My face numbs as the ice cold world around me spins.

His eyes widen, but when he steps back he looks murderous. "You still think I would hurt you?"

The spinning slows down as my lungs expand again. Of course he would hurt me—faeries are evil! I know they are!

But despite his ominous appearance, I just watched this faerie make himself sick to look after a human child. He didn't kill Liisa with his dance last night, and he made my sleep dreamless when they should have been full of nightmares. His behavior doesn't align with my grandmother's stories at all. "You do this every night?"

His green eyes bore into me. "Every night."

I can't help the way my heart softens around the edges at the passion in his voice. And just for a second, I let myself wonder what my life would be like now if I'd had a faerie stay with me after my grandmother died. Like Finn has.

As quick as the thought is there, I push it away. Nothing can change the past. And if I could change it, I'd still pick a safe home over magic.

But perhaps I still owe *this* faerie an explanation for my behavior yesterday. I rub my cold hands against my skirts. "I thought faerie dances killed humans. In..." I hesitate, swallowing down the unease of his unnerving attention. "In the tale my grandmother told me, a faerie danced a girl to death for stealing the butter lump from his porridge."

He snorts. "Is that why you ruined our fun last night?"

I nod, and he shakes his head as if I'm more of a lost cause than he imagined. *I might be.* But I've never once been told a story where a faerie helped humans without selfish gain, so what else was I to believe? I prop my fists on my hips. "How was I supposed to know you weren't killing her?"

His eyes widen. "You slept in a bed with me, and I didn't kill you, did I?"

I swallow, and my voice loses its edge. "No. You helped me."

He narrows his eyes. "I can see now that was a mistake."

My blood turns cold, and fear tingles at the edges of my vision. "What?"

Is this when he'll show his true colors? I brace for whatever he will do, but his attention is on the skeletal tree shadow next to us, not on me. "Clearly, kindness is wasted on you."

"How can you say that when—" But before I finish my sentence, he disappears in thin air. And he didn't hurt me.

I let out a relieved breath.

But as soon as the fear leaves, anger takes its place.

I'm not wrong about this. Why would there be stories to warn people against the faeries if they weren't masters at manipulating human emotion? And what better way for him to gain my trust than to help me with my nightmares? No, he might not have hurt Liisa last night, or me the one before, but that doesn't mean I can trust him.

I trudge back towards the cabin through the frozen landscape. The cold seeps through my shirt sleeves now that I'm no longer focused on Cian, and I wrap my arms around my middle to stave off the shivers.

A flickering light through the green windowpane on the second floor of my neighbor's home stops me in my tracks. Finn.

How could I forget about him? I might carry the grief of my own helplessness all those years ago. But what is that ache worth if I can't help him now? The faeries never came for me, and I don't know how long this one will stick around.

But I can still be to Finn what I never had.

Two days later, the full moon bathes the Northwoods in silver light. It glints off the graying temples of the man who pulls his tired horse along as it hauls the staggered bundles of kindling home. Dances over the group of children huddled together as they trudge through the snow. Lights the exasperated expression on a merchant's face as he argues with a townsman.

The winter night is clear and beautiful—maybe too beautiful to be wasted on the anger still simmering in my chest from talking to the faerie in the hollow.

I point my skis in a vee to make my way up the hill to my house. My heavy steps ease off as I reach the crest of the hill, and I falter a little as I face the door.

Liisa and I haven't talked after our fight, and it's the first time we've been alone since that night. Without Ingerid as our buffer, I'm not sure how it will go. I unstrap my skis and lean them up against the wall. The door creaks as warmth from the room licks at my frozen face. I push the door closed behind me and tug off my mittens and shawls.

Liisa dances into the room, but when she sees me, her shoulders stiffen, and she stops short. "Saoirse."

Her voice is not the cheerful one I usually hear when I come home, and my chest aches at the loss of her sunshine. "Liisa, I'm sorry."

She shrugs. "I'm not your keeper. If you want to hide every attached man in town in your bedroom it's not my business, is it?"

I wince at the harshness in her voice. "I don't trust Cian, and I was worried he'd hurt you."

Her eyebrows rise. "Right." She wouldn't be so suspicious if I could tell her the whole truth, but I can't. The less she knows, the safer she'll be.

I kick my boots off. "I would never intentionally hurt you, I hope you know that."

"Let's agree to disagree." She crosses the floor and gives the stew in the iron pot a stir. "I haven't eaten yet, and Ingerid won't be home for a while."

The ache in my heart eases a little. Liisa might not have forgiven me, but at least she's not ready to make me eat alone. I pull down my bowl and spoon from the wall and sit down on the long bench next to her. Who knew I'd miss our table this much?

We eat in silence. I'm starving, and with the way Liisa scarfs down the food, she must be too. She holds her bowl to her mouth to catch the last drops of stew, then drops it to her lap. Her gaze narrows on me. "Did you know they're celebrating Ingerid and Erkki at the tavern tonight?"

I put my spoon down. "Yes, I heard. Are you going?"

She swallows, and a look of vulnerability flits across her features. "If you are?"

She's no longer looking at me, but my heart feels light all the same. "Yes. You want me to help you braid your hair the way you like?"

She looks up then, and a real smile curls her lips. "I'd love that."

A half hour later, we make our way down to the tavern on foot. The hill is slick with hardened snow, and both Liisa and I slip several times. We have no choice but to hold onto each other to keep upright, and by the time we make it down the hill, we're both laughing. And my heart feels lighter than it has since I first saw the faerie in the hollow.

The tavern is already crowded, and raucous laughter fills every corner of the room. The rapid melody that careens through the air tugs at my feet, tempting them to dance.

The fiddler is perched on a table, his sweat-dropped brow furrowed in concentration as a smile tugs at his lips. His coat is tossed to the side, and he's dressed only in a shirt and trousers held up with colorful suspenders. His body moves in a dance of its own as his bow dips and rises swiftly across the strings.

Around him, boots tap the floor and dark skirts swirl up around the dancing couples, revealing stockings and petticoats in reds and blues. I see Kari Bakken wrapped around a man I don't recognize. His hands dive into her honey-blonde curls while they kiss as if there's an air shortage. I don't even waste an eye roll.

"Oh, I really like this one." Liisa sways in time with the music, and in another moment she's laughing at a boy pulling her into a dance. I twirl to look for Ask, but I don't see him.

"A dance, miss?" Blue eyes sparkle as they take in mine, and I can't help but return Erkki's friend's smile. I take his hand and let him tug me onto the floor. It's still early, and I only promised Ask one of my dances tonight.

TOO MUCH RED currant wine sloshes in my stomach. The flickering lamplight in the room has long since collected into glittering lines that swirl every time I move. I lean up against a wall and enjoy the way the room spins around me.

"A bright future for the happy couple." The shout comes from nowhere and everywhere all at once. I think.

I raise my jug with the rest of the crowd in the tavern while I look for my sister and her soon-to-be husband—careful not to move my head so fast I fall. A blue shirt waist and golden braids catch my eye. I look closer and see two Ingerids perched on Erkki's lap.

I squint.

No, there's only one. One Ingerid and one Erkki, with eyes for none but each other. They're likely the soberest people in the tavern since each time another toast is made, their kisses last longer—they've forgotten more than once to sip from their jugs after. I have not forgotten any sips.

An arm snakes around my waist and a sloppy kiss is planted on my neck. I let out a squeal and turn around. The lights follow a moment later, and brown, slightly hazy eyes meet mine. I grab his biceps to keep myself steady, my lips tilting up into a smile. "Ask?"

The man of my dreams grins—a stupid, lopsided grin. He presses another kiss to my temple and tugs me closer to his large body. The scent of his last sip of ale is still etched into his words. "You're so pretty."

The way he jostles me brings another wave of nausea. How much have I had to drink? Bile tickles the back of my throat. *Too much. Definitely too much.* There's no way I can still dance with him. Just the thought of intentional movement makes my stomach roil.

And where is Liisa? We came here together, and I ought to have kept track of her, but I don't remember where she is. "I need to find Liisa."

"Hmm?" Ask grunts, but he makes no move to let me go.

I tug on his big arm, but it's too heavy. The music is so loud, and whenever it stills, the dissatisfied roar of the crowd brings it back.

I rest my head on his broad chest. I'm exhausted, I should probably try to sleep a bit before I go find Liisa. And the coat pressed against my cheek is soft and smells like… earth and fire. Like Ask.

I close my eyes and breathe him in.

"I can't meet you tomorrow." His breath tastes spicy, like the ale he's been drinking. But then his words sink in, and my heart flops to the bottom of my stomach.

"You can't?"

He shakes his head, and the motion makes my insides spin. I curl my hand a little tighter around his arm as disappointment courses through my blood, mixing with the wine. He doesn't like me that way—I ought to have known.

I pull away a bit, but he doesn't even seem to notice, and my heart does another disappointed twirl in my chest.

Ask nuzzles my jaw with his nose. "Meet me the day after? At the smithy?"

My skin trembles under his touch, and it takes me a second to comprehend his words. He does want me! My heart picks up its beat, and my childhood dream is so close it feels as if I can reach out and touch it. "When?" I sound too eager, but I can't help it.

His chuckle tickles my ear. "Early. Whenever. I'll be there all day."

I tuck close to him again with a happy sigh. Ask wants to see me! My grin stretches my cheeks, and I don't care that my eyes hurt and my head aches, because someday soon I'll have my safe home. Maybe I'll even be able to help Finn?

Silly grin still on my face, I let the sounds of the party lull me until my eyes shut—just for a minute.

I don't know how much time has passed when someone bumps into me again. "Saoirse?" Liisa's voice is loud in my ear.

I wince. "Don't scream."

Liisa laughs even louder, and I whimper as the sound reverberates through my skull. Then she tugs me away from Ask, who somehow doesn't protest. She looks slightly blurry as she peers into my eyes. "Saints, how much did you have to drink?"

I hold up two fingers. They're supposed to stay the same distance apart, but they don't. A man laughs close by, and the rich sound makes heat curl in my stomach. Ask?

Strong arms that are not Liisa's wrap around me and heft me up against a hard chest. But when I find my captors face, no lopsided grin meets me. All I get is an exaggerated eye roll from green eyes much too beautiful to belong to a man. "Struggling with your drink, human?"

I frown, but it doesn't seem to make me any smarter. "I'm not."

He doesn't comment, but I don't care what he has to say. His grip behind my back and under my knees is warm, and I rest my cheek against the rhythmic heartbeat under his shirt.

A door slams and the crowd quiets. It's easier to breathe, but the air entering my lungs is freezing. I snuggle closer to the warm body cradling me.

"It's so cold." My teeth are chattering so hard I can barely get the words out.

"Tends to be that in mid-winter." He jostles me again, and the wind picks up. The uneven rocking as he stomps through the snow seems to go on forever. Then he stops, and suddenly my boots hit the ground.

I sway as bile rises in my throat. "I—" I clamp a hand to my mouth, and next thing I know, I'm leaning over a piece of wood. The railing by our door?

I think it is, but I can't think too long on it when every stupid cup of red currant wine burns as it comes back up. A warm hand at my neck keeps my braids away from the mess. Surely not the faerie's?

The painful retching finally ends, and I'm jostled around again. The world is nothing but a haze until I'm lowered into a bed with straw that rustles softly as I turn my cheek into the pillow. Stiff, clean sheets caress my bare toes, and a man's dark timbre sounds in the hallway. Liisa laughs softly in response to whatever he says.

At least I think it's Liisa.

The door closes, and a hand tugs my blanket up to my chin. I snuggle deeper into my pillow and don't bother to open my eyes to see whose hand it is.

I know whose I want it to be. "I could have used some of that magic when I was younger, you know."

"Is that so?" Cian's voice is silk against my nerve endings. So smooth and warm, I want to drink it like honeyed milk. Or curl up under it like with a blanket.

"Mhmm. I wouldn't have had to grow up so fast." I dig my toes into the mattress, and straw crunches under the sheet.

"Why did you?" His breath washes over my face, and no spicy scent of alcohol tickles my senses. Do faeries not drink, or is this one just the sober kind?

"So I could stay out of my aunt's way when she was angry."

"Did that work?" His voice is quiet, as if he knows what he speaks of. But he doesn't, does he?

A chuckle colors my voice, but there's no warmth there. "No. But running away did. I had to when the magic folk weren't going to save me." They *were* just as evil as in my grandmother's stories. Cian is only here tonight, helping me because....

But my head feels like it's about to split in two, so I give up on trying to remember why he's here. It doesn't change anything.

"Is that why you hate me so much?" His voice curls around me, tucking me under the blankets. Or is that his hands?

"Wouldn't you—" I hiccup. "Hate what could have saved you, but didn't?"

He doesn't answer. Is he gone already? I want to check, but my eyelids are so heavy.

Warm fingers brush gently against my cheek.

It can't be Cian, but the hand is larger than Liisa's, and she's never smelled like midnight air and distant spruce woods. The hand disappears, and I immediately miss the warm caress—it's been so long since anyone stroked my cheek.

I wait for him to speak, but he doesn't. "Are you a cat now?"

His chuckle fills the dark beyond my eyelids. "No, but I will be soon."

I wiggle my toes to get the blood moving. "For Finn?"

"Yes, for Finn."

I let out a deep breath, and snuggle even deeper under the blanket. "That's good."

The next time I stir, bright sunlight burns through my eyelids, and the clatter of wooden bowls is like a hammer to my skull. And Cian is gone.

CHAPTER 11

I f I never taste red currant wine again, it will be too soon. My head pounds as I walk home from the Pedersen farm. I still can't resist tilting my head back to watch the northern lights paint the skies. The night is so still and cold, even the people that trek through the streets are quiet—their voices muffled under scarves and hoods.

Then someone bumps into me from behind, intensifying the throbbing at my temples. "Maybe watch the road, not the sky, miss." I don't recognize the gruff voice, but I do step over to a spot where I'm less likely to get bowled over. When I get my fill of the sharp green ribbons undulating above me, I start on the slick hillside leading towards home. At the top of the hill, torch-light flickers over a figure on the stone steps in the alley. Finn lifts his hand in a timid wave and gives me a hesitant smile.

I turn towards him with a grin, ignoring my throbbing skull. The snow crunches under my boots as I step close enough to plop down next to him.

I frown at the dark-striped tabby. Didn't he say that staying a cat for too long wore him out? It's close to night time, so shouldn't he be sick already?

Finn's wide green eyes catch mine. "You made my cat all better."

I shake my head. "He did that himself, I just gave him a place to rest."

The tabby leaves Finn's side and rubs itself against my stocking-clad calves.

Cian is rubbing his face against my legs.

I squeal, and clamp my skirts down around my ankles. *Cursed faerie!* He looks up at me, and I swear he's laughing.

Finn wrinkles his nose, and tucks a lock of dark blonde hair back under his knit cap. "Are you not very used to cats?"

I blush. Of course, that would be what he thinks, and I can't tell him otherwise. "No. Um, I've never had a cat."

"They're very nice." The cat leaves my side, apparently done torturing me, and shoves his head into Finn's little mittened palm instead. The wind is cold, and I'm just about to say my goodbyes and head inside for supper, when Finn cries out. "My cat!"

I turn so fast my neck burns only to see the cat slumped on the steps. Another faerie trick? But Finn is hysterical, and as much as I don't trust Cian to be honest with me, I don't think he'd frighten Finn like this for fun.

Big tears roll down the boy's cheeks as he sobs. "He's dead!"

I put my hand to the cat's warm underside and find the gentle rise and fall of each invisible breath. "He's breathing, love. He's not dead."

Finn swipes at his eyes then gasps as he glances towards the road. "I need to get him to my room before Master Johannes comes home. He won't like this!" The panic in his voice makes my heart bleed.

"Here. I'll help you." I heft the tabby up into my arms, and let Finn lead the way into the cabin. I follow him through rooms arranged much like the ones next door. The similarities end there, however. Where the thick, timbered walls in our house smell like Ingerid's cooking, with air that always brims with laughter, this house smells like stale ale and filth.

I cringe as I follow Finn up the stairs to his small room. I don't think the rough floor boards have seen a broom in a long time, and certainly not a good scrubbing. The sheets on his bed, too, look like they need a wash, and the straw mattress is flat from long use. My aunt's house was at least clean.

"Put him here." Finn pulls a worn woven blanket over his unkempt bed, and I put the cat down. Finn crouches next to him and rests his head next to the sleeping cat. Teary-eyed, he begs me to make Cian better, and I don't think I've understood until now just how much the faerie's presence means to Finn.

My misguided belief in the magic folk one day showing up to save me kept me sane during my years with my aunt. But it's clear that to Finn, that saving grace is Cian's presence.

"He'll be all right." I sink to the dingy floor, keeping my palm on the cat's back to make sure it's still breathing—that my words are not lies. I don't know how long I've knelt there when the door slams downstairs.

The color drains from Finn's face. "Master Johannes. He can't find you here."

I nod. "I'll hide." Finn looks so scared, I'd promise him anything right now. I look around for a hiding spot, but Finn's glance to the tabby on the bed makes me amend my promise. "With the cat." I cradle the small animal to my chest as heavy boots thump on the stairs.

Finn shoves aside a chest and opens the doors to a small closet. "In here, quick."

I move into the dark space, holding tight to the cat and hoping against hope that there aren't vermin hiding in this place. The door closes and I have no choice but to breathe in the musty smell.

Outside the closed door, the chest scrapes across the floor, and Finn grunts as he shoves it back in place. His uncle calls his name, Finn rushes out of the room, and I'm alone.

Well, almost alone.

I tuck myself against the back wall and pull my legs up under my skirts. My stomach growls. It's been hours since I last ate. How long will I be stuck here? I don't want to get Finn in trouble with his uncle, which will certainly happen if I just traipse out of here.

I look down at the sleeping cat in my lap. Or at least I hope he's still asleep. There's no way for me to know if he's all right or not.

The door creaks and light footsteps tap across the floor.

"Mistress Saoirse?" Finn's whisper works its way through the closet door.

"I'm here." As if I'd be anywhere else with a wooden chest shoved in front of my hiding spot.

"Master Johannes isn't asleep yet, I can hear him downstairs." The last word breaks off on a yawn, and he sniffs. The bed frame creaks, and the straw mattress rustles. It has to be past Finn's bedtime.

"You can go to sleep, Finn. I'll be alright here with your cat." It's not quite the truth, but Finn is so young, and he needs his sleep. I'll just wait until his uncle falls asleep and try to sneak out then.

"Okay." Another yawn fills the air, then the rustling of fabric, another soft crackle of straw. And then, it's quiet.

Hours seem to pass while I sit in the dark, with only the distant jingles and creaks from the horse-drawn sleighs passing outside for company.

Then the cat in my lap suddenly burns against my thighs. A flash of lightning bathes the closet in light. I swallow a scream, and in the next second Cian's body awkwardly covers mine. He curses quietly close to my ear but makes no effort to move.

"You are on top of me." I speak the words into his hair while the silky strands tickle my dry lips.

"Yes, I know." His breaths are labored as if simply speaking the words takes considerable effort.

I hate the way he feels pressed against me, but I don't hate it anywhere near enough. My heart beats faster. "Are you going to do anything to change that?"

He huffs a breath. "Human, I'm trying so hard not to puke my guts out all over you, so give me a minute, will you?"

I shudder at the image and try to straighten to put space between his chest and mine, but all that seems to do is the opposite. His heart pounds against mine, and my blood heats against my will.

"Been a while since we did this, huh?" His breath is warm against my neck, and goosebumps rise across my skin. His lips stretch in a smile against my jaw. "It's not too bad?"

His voice shouldn't affect me, but it does, and the timbre in it sends a delicious tingle down my spine. When his fingers find mine on the floor, his touch is like the living glow of a sunrise. Like the stillness after a thunderstorm.

Sweet. Intoxicating. Pure.

Like magic.

The dark closet shrinks around us, and I feel Cian *everywhere*. The heat of his body surrounds me as if I'm inside *him*, not just this closet. I can't help it when my lips brush the warm skin of his neck, tasting him. The air around us thickens with desire, and the breath he pulls in is sharp. "You can't kiss me."

I still. Did he just say what I think he said? Who does he think he is?

I press my head to the closet's back wall, as far away from him as I can get, but it's nowhere near far enough. "I don't want to kiss you."

His dark chuckle swirls through the air, over my skin,

leaving trails of magic in its wake. "You've wanted to kiss me since the day I broke your table."

My cheeks heat, but with embarrassment this time. "Have not." Why would I want to kiss a faerie? I've heard enough stories to know any attraction between us is just the effect of his magic. It isn't real.

"You know human desire is visible to faeries, right?"

My stomach drops. Surely he's jesting? "No, it's not."

He snorts. "It is. And yours just went out like a flame under a bucket of water."

He's not wrong, but that could have been a lucky guess, right? Who *would* still feel desire after what he just said? I clear my throat, hating the tremble in my voice. "None of that means I want to kiss you, or ever wanted to."

His grin is a living thing in the dark, evil and obnoxious. "You know it does. And before you do something stupid like kiss me to prove me wrong, you need to know that faerie kisses are fatal to humans."

That's definitely not true. I roll my eyes. "Right, so out of the goodness of your heart, you want to protect me from an agonizing death? How sweet." I laugh, but there's no mirth in the sound.

"There's nothing funny about this. Humans who kiss a faerie who doesn't love them become obsessed." His chiding voice bites into my wounded pride, and I can't hold back my snort.

"If you're worried I'll become obsessed with you, you have nothing to fear. I'm not—"

"And it's their obsession that kills them." His ominous words make the air inside the closet hard to breathe.

"And if they love each other?" I want to pull the words back before they've fully left my tongue. *Why would you ask that, Saoirse?*

But Cian stays quiet, and it's answer enough. Faeries don't

love—at least not humans. And it's no skin off my back. It's not like I'd want him to love *me*.

I'd pull farther away from him if I could, but there is no space. And I can't leave the closet. Not yet. Not when there's a chance Finn's uncle will find us in his nephew's room.

"Are you not able to shift?" Explaining a full grown man hanging out in a closet will be harder than explaining away a cat.

Cian groans. "God, no. I need rest first."

"So we're stuck here?"

He mumbles something I don't catch and sags against me. I push on his shoulders and whisper-yell at him to get off me, but he's dead weight.

Great! I'm stuck in a closet with a passed out faerie—just how I wanted to spend my evening. My stomach growls again, and I picture the bowl of stew waiting for me at home.

It's going to be a long night.

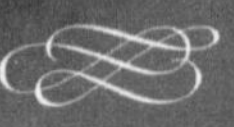

CHAPTER 12

The door to Finn's room creaks like a final bell toll, and my eyes fly open. When did I fall asleep? And what is Finn's uncle doing here?

But as terror holds me still, I listen more closely. The door shutting is only accompanied by light footsteps—Finn's. And then another sound breaks through my foggy mind. A horse's snort, and a jingling harness. Loud voices down on the street.

It's morning.

I try to sit up, but something heavy prevents me from moving. My eyes adjust to the sliver of moonlight that bursts through the crack between the closed closet doors, and I look down.

Cian's head rests in my lap, his long legs folded against the side wall. My face grows hot.

I've spent the entire night in a closet with a faerie, and in the most improper way possible. If there's a *proper* way to spend the night in a closet with a faerie when you're trying to convince a blacksmith's son to make you his wife.

How did last night's disagreement end with Cian asleep in

my lap? What is wrong with me? How could I do this to myself? To Ask?

I pound Cian's wide shoulders with my palm, but he doesn't stir. "Wake up, you oaf!"

He grunts, and snuggles against me.

I squeal, my face on fire.

His eyes spring open, gaze hazy and confused. "What's wrong?" His voice, hoarse with sleep, tugs at my insides, and blood rushes hotly through my veins.

I push at his giant frame. "Get out of my lap!"

A wolfish grin spreads across his face, clearing the sleep from his eyes. "Well well, little human. What's this predicament you've found yourself in?"

"*I'm* not doing anything wrong! It's not my fault that you fell asleep *on top of me*!"

His grin flashes in the half dark. "I'm pretty sure you were the one who snuggled up to me first."

My cheeks are on fire, and he's too close to slap. Not that slapping a faerie would be a wise decision. "I'm pretty sure I didn't. And if I did, I want you to move, now!"

"Of course, Mistress Saoirse." He sits up, but his grin doesn't fade. And neither does my rapid heart beat. I curl my hands into fists lest they get any other ideas—like sliding under the shirt that strains over his shoulders. "Remember what I told you about human desire?"

I shake my head. There's no way he can really see desire. And if he did, there'd be nothing to see. Nothing at all.

Cian's gaze follows the outline of my lips, then drops to where my pulse is speeding into a gallop. In the half light, his green eyes darken to black. "You want me."

I swallow and lie. "I don't."

He opens his mouth to respond when a door slams downstairs. The sound reverberates through the cabin, through my bones. I hold perfectly still for a second, two, three, but all is quiet.

And even if it wasn't, I'm not staying another second in this closet. I'll chance getting discovered by Finn's uncle if it means getting away from Cian's stupid smirk. I scowl at him. "I don't want you, and if I did, I'd pick safety over fickle magic any day."

He snorts. "This again? How can you hold a grudge against me personally for something that happened when you were a child?"

I push to my feet, stumble out through the doors, and squeeze past the chest on the other side. Too tired from another night of not enough sleep, my boot catches on my skirts, and my face speeds towards the filthy floorboards in Finn's room.

Cian's strong fingers clamp around my arm and pull me back to standing. Blood rushes through my veins at his touch, but I tug my arm out of his hand as soon as I'm upright.

He chuckles. "You're welcome."

I don't respond. I need to get away from him. Now.

He follows me down the stairs, his whisper-shout loud behind me. "You're kind of crabby in the mornings, you know that?"

I turn to nail him with a withering glare and a whisper-shout of my own. "Are you insane? Be quiet!"

Loud snores sound from the other room, and as we turn the corner Finn's uncle is sprawled on a bench, boots off and shirt unfastened. The table is covered in jugs. Suddenly I'm thankful to have spent the night in Finn's closet, even if it meant waking up in such an intimate position with Cian. If for nothing else, Finn wasn't alone.

We tiptoe past the bench. My boot sticks to the darkened floorboards next to an overturned crock. The whole downstairs smells like stale food and soured ale, and when we finally push through the door to the outside, I immediately pull in a deep breath of fresh air.

Unfortunately, my faerie company is still here, clouding the frozen air with his own scent.

I prop my hands on my waist. "You can leave now."

He mimics my stance, and I'm willing to bet mine doesn't make me look near as irresistible as his does. Cian's shirt pulls across his broad chest, and his dark blonde hair looks like someone has been running their fingers through it all night. Tugging. Pulling. My hands tighten into fists, and my face warms as I hope desperately it's not my own work.

His full lips pull into a smirk. "Why are you in such a hurry for me to leave? Do you have plans to meet *a suitor*?"

My eyes narrow. How does he know I'm meeting Ask? "I do in fact."

The teasing tone disappears from his voice, replaced by an emotion I can't quite place. Disgust? Condescension? "Really, a blacksmith's son is the best you can do? Is he your *safe* choice?" He spits the word *safe* as if it's personally offended him.

I bristle. "There's nothing wrong with being a blacksmith's wife."

His eyes narrow. "It is when he's not what you want."

"You don't know anything about what I want!"

He steps close until he towers over me, until my breath is wrapped in the tantalizing scent of spruce woods and midnight. "But I know that your heart beat faster in that closet with me than it's done anytime you've talked about becoming that boy's wife."

He tilts his head as if to lean in for a kiss, and my stomach tightens. But he can't kiss me. Unless his warning last night was a lie? *Because faeries aren't known for lying, Saoirse.*

I swallow, my throat suddenly desperate for moisture.

His breath feathers across my lips. "I know you want to kiss me." *Kiss.* The word slithers through the air like the hiss of a viper, ready to bite.

Startled, I pull away.

He laughs, and my face burns.

Without another word, I turn and walk away. Cian might have saved me from an even worse hangover when he carried me home from the tavern the night before last. But that doesn't mean he *is* safe. It doesn't mean magic is any safer a choice than it was when I was a child.

He's a faerie, Saoirse. You're nothing but a human toy to him.

And I can't forget it again.

CHAPTER 13

A gasp sounds as I push through the door, and it takes my eyes a second to adjust to the dark interior of the cabin.

Ingerid is bundled up in her hood and scarves, but she makes no move towards the door. Her gaze rakes over me. "Where were you? I can't believe you stayed out all night!"

"I'm sure she wasn't actually *outside*, Ingerid." The chill in Liisa's words rivals the snowy world beyond the door. Avoiding my gaze, she slips her mittens on and slides past me to leave.

"I needed to talk to Cian and we fell asleep, that's all."

Ingerid looks unconvinced, but there's no time for her to argue, she's waited too long for me to show up already. She wraps another shawl around her neck and shakes her head. "Please don't do it again. I was so worried about you."

I follow her out the door. A quick glance down the darkened alley between my cabin and Finn's, is all I dare, but no shadows move over the snowy blanket. The hollow is empty.

Which is just as well. I might find Cian attractive, and the memory of his hot breath on my neck might burn my cheeks despite the cool winter air. But he'll never be a safe choice. He'll never be able to give me the life Ask can.

I walk through town in the dark, my boots moving sound-lessly through the powdery snow. The sun is hours from rising, but the town already bustles with activity. Women wrapped up in shawls and hoods pull carts and carry bundles of firewood. A group of men are gathered at a street corner, their argument loud and heated. A little boy pushes past me, twisting his neck to watch for the girl hot on his trail. Their cheeks are rosy, and their laughter floats like puffs of smoke in the freezing air.

The tarred buildings where Ask's father makes his living are set away from the rest of the town for obvious reasons. The scorching fires needed to meld iron are given no opportunity to reach the wooden homes and outbuildings of the farms nearby.

The air here seems warmer. It smells different, too, a bit like Ask. And then the man I'm here to meet bends low to avoid the beam of the doorway. He straightens, and his eyes light as he sees me.

"You came." His grin is the lopsided one he gave me at the party two nights ago. The one that should make my stomach flutter wildly with butterflies, but doesn't.

Yet.

I slip my hand out of my mitten and into his large calloused one and let him pull me behind a partition in his father's stables —a space perfectly suited for one purpose and one purpose only. And if the way Ask's eyes darken is any indication, it's one of which I'm very much in favor.

Memories of my night with Cian crowd my mind, pulling me out of the moment.

"You can't kiss me."

"I don't want to kiss you."

"You've wanted to kiss me since the day I broke your table."

My pulse quickens—heating my cheeks, and making my stomach flutter as if I'm right back in the closet with a faerie draped across me.

"I want to kiss you, Saoirse." Ask's husky voice drags me

back to the present. The sweet scent of hay filters up from under our feet, blending with that of iron and ashes.

Cian sneers in my memory.

"Is he your safe choice?"

"There's nothing wrong with being a blacksmith's wife."

"It is when he's not what you want."

I push Cian's words out of my head. He doesn't know what I want. He's a faerie. He can't possibly understand how desperately I've fought to get back to the safe haven that was taken from me at eleven. *How much I need this kiss, this relationship, to happen.*

Ask's rough hands slide along my jaw, and I pull in a sharp breath. The heat of his body collides with mine, and a smile tilts his lips, making a dimple pop in his cheek. Then he leans in.

Fire burns my lips, and I scream.

My eyes pop open in time to see Ask's confused gaze roam over my face. Except the creature pressed up against me looks nothing like Ask. His face bulges as his nose turns into a hideous snout.

I jump back, lips still on fire, and my back hits the wall behind me with a thump.

A man swears on the other side of the wall, and Ask's eyes light with anger. "What did you think I was going to do?"

His hot whisper is meant for me, I think, but his father bellows his name all the same. "You have work to do, son, you can pick up with that tart later."

A flush heats my neck, and I want to shrink into nothing. Ask's nose no longer looks like a snout, and my lips are no longer on fire. Did I imagine it?

"It...burned." Embarrassment makes bile rise in my throat.

Ask rolls his eyes. "You could have just said no. I know I didn't hurt you." He stomps away, and I slink out the door. Iron strikes iron again behind me, and the clatter of wooden buckets fills the air. Whatever just happened, my time with Ask is over for now.

If not forever.

Presumably, there are other girls for him to drag behind that partition wall that won't suddenly imagine him beastlike and pull away. Other girls happy to take my place in the safe home he has to offer.

I stomp through the frozen town. Too focused on what happened at the smithy, I almost run headfirst into the last man I want to see. He's too tall, too slender, and not at all safe.

Cian's green eyes take in my flushed skin as if it's the most delightful thing he's seen all day. "Now where have you been, little human girl?"

My hand tightens into a fist. I can't deal with an obnoxious faerie, not after what just happened. "Go away, Cian."

He shakes his head and tsks. "So grizzly. Did your meeting with your true love not go so well? Or is that your *safe* love?" His cheerful tone slips just a bit on the word safe.

My face heats. I messed up what would have been my first kiss with Ask, and I don't even understand how it happened. "It's none of your business."

My words are clipped, but the faerie's eyes sparkle as he takes in my red face. He opens his mouth to speak, but doesn't get the chance when I brush past him and walk back up the hill.

Just because I woke up in a hall closet with him, doesn't mean I owe him any details about my personal life. We are not friends. He is only a faerie.

THE FIRE CRACKLES in the hearth, and the sweet scent wafting up from our work should make the room cozy, but all I feel is the sting of Ask's rejection. I can't concentrate on poking my needle through the fresh fruit slices any more than I can forget Ask's hideous face earlier. I've drawn blood from my pointer finger twice, and I wince as it happens for the third time.

"What's gotten into you?" Ingerid sends me yet another concerned look.

But when I cave and tell her the humiliating story, she only looks more worried. "His lips *burned* you?" She drops her half-finished apple slice garland and stares at me as if *I'm* the one whose face just turned into a snout.

"Yes! As soon as we kissed, my lips felt like they were on fire, and when I looked at him, his skin was all red and weird, and his nose was growing."

I reach for my mulled wine, clutching the warm stoneware mug to my chest, but the heat doesn't comfort. I'd thought Ingerid would understand, maybe even have some advice—she's about to be married after all. But her reaction has me feeling stupider than ever.

Ingerid frowns as she puts her needle safely away, then pulls her knees up to her chest to rest her chin on them. "I thought you wanted to kiss Ask."

I choke on my wine, and cough. "I do!"

"Then I don't understand how that could happen?"

"Wait, I'm confused!" I replay her words, but they make me no wiser. "How would that happen if I didn't want to kiss him?"

"Um, I mean, it wouldn't really." Ingerid's gaze is intent on her hand rifling through the pile of garlands. My stomach sinks, and my hand drops to let the mug rest on my thighs. "You don't believe me?"

Her guilty eyes meet mine. "No! I believe you. I believe you suddenly felt as if your lips burned, and that Ask looked disgusting to you. I just don't. I mean, I don't understand how his face could change like that."

That makes two of us.

"Maybe you're cursed." Liisa tilts her head to the side and

watches me carefully from her perch on the sheepskin on the wooden bench. It's her first contribution to the conversation, but I know she's heard every word. "Did you try to kiss anyone else?"

Goosebumps break out across my chest as I remember the charged air between me and Cian this morning, and my cheeks heat. "No."

But the answer is too quick, and by the glint in Liisa's eyes, she notices, too. She gasps and throws an apple slice at me. "Who? I thought you were supposed to be head over heels with Ask. And yet you stay out all night with, and kiss, other men?"

I pop the apple slice in my mouth. "I *am* head over heels with Ask! And I didn't kiss anyone else." But suddenly I can't push away the images from Finn's closet—Cian's breath over my lips, his chest pressed against mine.

"Then why is your face so red? Did he too turn into a beast?" Liisa's tone is a little more mocking than it ought to be. Has she *really* forgiven me for breaking up her and Cian's dance that night?

I groan. "No, he didn't. And—"

But then her earlier words sink in, and one thing is very clear in my mind.

Cian. I'd run into Cian after leaving Ask. What if the faerie's good mood was because he'd cursed our kiss?

But why would Cian thwart my relationship with Ask?

But the question is as ludicrous as my getting involved with a magic being in the first place. Of course, he'd find a way to curse my kiss. Faeries love to mess with humans.

That filthy, jealous… faerie! I'm going to throttle him!

I push up from the bench. "Sorry, I just remembered I need to do something."

"Liisa, did you really need to say that?" Ingerid's voice is full of chiding.

"Say what? I didn't say anything!"

I ignore their squabble and reach for my shawl hanging from the hook by the door. Behind Ingrid and Liisa is an exact replica of our old table. "When did we get a new table?"

Liisa turns around. "When did that get there? Was it there when you came in?"

"No." Surely, I would have noticed a new table when I walked in after my failure of a kiss?

"I didn't notice it either." Ingerid looks to me. "Did Cian bring that?"

I shake my head, though he probably did. If he thinks I'll see a new table as an apology for turning my bethrothed into a beast, he's sorely mistaken. Leaving the shawl on the hook, I push through the door and into the cold, dark winter day.

I stomp through the snow, and in less than a minute, the hollow stretches before me. "Cian!" My angry voice fills the air, and the names I call him are quick to follow. I'm halfway through his actual name for the second time when he appears, all flawless beauty and golden skin. But his looks can't save him now.

Not even the grin that tumbles my stomach.

I prop my hands on my hips and force the flutters in my chest to still. "I can't believe you'd try to ruin my future like that! You know how much I need him!"

His grin slips a little. "What was that now, little human? Why would you need a boring blacksmith when there's magic to be had?"

There isn't magic to be had! And if there was, why would I want it? Why, when the mere existence of magic thwarts my happiness at every turn?

I cross my arms and stomp my foot. I don't care how childish it makes me look. "You can keep your stupid magic to yourself. I don't want it, and I don't need it!"

He looks at me as if my anger is adorable, and I want nothing more than to wipe the smug expression off his face. I close the distance between us until the heat of his body blasts against mine.

"I know all about the magic you have to offer, and it wasn't *enough*—" My voice breaks on the last word. Every painful moment following my grandmother's death weighs down on me like an iron blanket. Too heavy to move under, too heavy for the cold air to reach my lungs.

"You don't know what it's like to be all alone in the world and have your trust stolen too. I needed the magic in those stories to save me, and they didn't."

His face is like a storm cloud in the half-dark. "And you think that's reason enough to hate me? To judge the character of my people? Because an old woman's stories didn't save you from losing her?"

I scoff and swipe at the errant tear escaping my lashes. "No. Not because I lost her. Because I lost my belief that someone would save me. I needed them to come for me, and they didn't."

The air between us turns even colder, and I remember why I'm here. "And now, you're determined to ruin my chance to have that life back."

His jaw is tight. "What are you getting at?" Even angry, he looks too beautiful, too much like the magical faerie he is.

"You cursed Ask! You're the reason his lips burned and his face turned beast-like when he kissed me!"

His shocked laughter can't hide the sparkle of mischief in his eyes. "Oh, love, I hate to be the bearer of bad news, but if kissing him makes him look like a beast, you're not as smitten as you think you are."

I growl and clench my hands at my sides. Stupid, infuriating faerie! "That's not why it happened, and you know it! How dare you use your magic on my betrothed?"

A frown appears on Cian's forehead, and damn if it doesn't make him look even more attractive. Why couldn't my grandmother have been right about the faeries' sheer ugliness, too?

"Did he ask you to marry him? After you refused to kiss him?"

Remembering Ask's curt dismissal, I falter. "No, he didn't."

"Then he's not your betrothed, is he?" Cian's tone is all challenge, and I hate that he's right.

But I'm right, too. "He *would* have asked me, if you hadn't magicked him."

Cian laughs again, and it echoes off the frozen trees around us, cold and callous—just like him. Just like his people. "I wouldn't be so sure, little human."

I launch forward, but before I can touch him, much less throttle him—he is gone.

CHAPTER 14

The week passes blissfully faerie-free while the three of us hem sheets for Ingrid's bridal chest until our fingertips are raw and our eyes ache from squinting. But on a particularly frosty day, my luck runs out.

Of course, he's picked a time when both Ingerid and Liisa are out. Without invitation he takes a seat on the bench by the table I assume he procured. If he's waiting for me to mention it —or worse, thank him!—he'll have to wait a long time.

But Cian doesn't say a word. He just watches me—his gaze so intense my mouth goes dry.

I turn to stir the soup on the hearth that absolutely doesn't need stirring. I've kept an eye on it just fine until the faerie showed up, but I'll take any excuse to avoid making conversation. The warm, earthy aroma that wafts up from the pot fills the air in the room, making my mouth water.

"You know, human, your strangely obstinate choice of safety over magic would be admirable if it wasn't rooted in cowardice." His melodious voice makes a delightful shiver sprint down my spine.

I roll my eyes as I look through the spice chest. Ingerid is an excellent cook, and the soup needs nothing. I, however, desperately need a distraction from the faerie haunting me. "Such sweet words, no wonder you have women falling all over you."

I catch his narrowed eyes out of the corner of my own. "I have more humans vying for my attention than *you* have."

I turn to him then, hands on hips and jaw tight. "And whose fault is that?" Ask hasn't spoken to me other than in passing since our disaster of a kiss. "I don't need *all* the humans to want my attention. Just one of them."

He scoffs. "Right, your safe choice."

I clench my hands in my skirts. "You say it as if it's a bad thing."

Cian's eyes widen, his hands flying out to his sides. "It *is* a bad thing! You don't even know what you're missing out on!"

"And I suppose you'll show me?" I hate the words as soon as they escape my lips. Why did I say that?

The corner of his mouth tilts up into a smirk that makes my breath hitch. His gaze trails from my eyes to my lips, then burns a path down to my collar bone. My skin heats as his gaze lingers, lowers... all the way down to the tips of my boots.

His attention snarls a band around my chest, and I can't breathe.

His eyes glitter darkly. "Tempting. But no." *Ouch.*

A faint knock sounds at the door. With a scathing glare at Cian, I cross the floor and fling it open.

"Miss Saoirse." Finn's voice is small, and before I know what's happened, Cian is beside me. He grinds out a curse, and flinches when a wide-eyed Finn draws back a step. But the boy doesn't know Cian as a man, and in this moment he looks nothing like a docile tabby. But there's no time to worry about that once I get a better look at Finn's face.

His cheekbone is mottled with purple.

The sight is a sucker punch, and I struggle to draw breath.

Somehow, I form words from the hollow inside me. "Did your uncle do this?"

Finn's attention is on the worn doorjamb. "I don't think he meant to."

My heart sinks at his need to defend the only family he knows. I know what it is like to tie your self-worth to the cruelty of those who were meant to love you.

But then I look at his face again, and I want to throttle the man who dared do this to a child in his care.

I reach for Finn with gentle hands. "Come. I'll make you some honey milk, and I think I might have some salve for that bruise." I force my voice to stay light, when all I want to do is figure out a way to get Finn away from his uncle. Forever.

Cian sits on a stool in the corner, a dark expression on his face. and I'm left to carry the forced conversation on my own. Liisa and Ingerid come home for supper and say nothing to Finn about his bruise, but Ingerid's eyes linger on it when Finn's attention is on his food. With a question in my eyes, I point to the jar of salve still on top of the chest, and she nods.

My heart aches as Finn leaves after supper. Why can't he stay? Why am I forced to return him to a man I know will hurt him again? If not with his fists, then surely with his anger?

Cian gets up from his stool and turns to me. "I need to leave. Can I talk to you first?"

Ingerid and Liisa exchange glances, and I know what they're thinking. But that's not why the faerie's asking to talk to me in private.

Or at least, I don't think it is.

I follow him out into the cold, starry night. The chill bites my nose and my fingers as the snow crunches under our boots. Only once we're nestled in the shadowed alley between my cabin and Finn's, does Cian speak.

"You." The word tumbles rough and husky off his lips, and I feel the impact down to my toes. Before I can ask what he means, his warm chest is flush against mine and he pushes me up against the chilled wall.

I pull in a breath of surprise. Whatever I expected from him when we walked out here, it wasn't this. And despite that, I can't find it in me to push him away.

For a long moment we hold still while our chests move in unison. But despite the heaving movement, actual air seems to elude my lungs. "I?"

He chuckles against my temple, and his lips—Did he just press a kiss to my skin?

But I can't think too long on that. Not when his nose traces a path down to my jaw, and my limbs liquify.

I clutch his strong shoulders. I don't pause to think. I can't think. My head swims as Cian's mouth explores my neck in the most delicious way. His scruff bites into the skin of my neck, and I never want him to stop.

His rough words skate over my jaw. "Seeing the rage in your eyes at what that devil did is the hottest thing I've ever seen."

Is he saying…?

"Me acting like a decent human being turns you on?" I pull in a ragged breath. "You must not get around much."

He grins against my collarbone, and his teeth nip my skin. "You'd be surprised."

I wouldn't, but I can't think why.

Not when his hands are roaming over my back, my arms, my waist. Definitely not as he pulls at my shirt sleeve and flicks the brooch at my throat till the pin breaks free.

Cold night air tickles my warm skin as he kisses my bare shoulder. "For someone who hates magic so desperately, the best parts of you are terribly magic." His whisper in my ear makes thousands of butterflies take off somewhere under my skin. I feel the flutter of their wings everywhere—just like I feel him *everywhere*.

"Cian."

He makes a sound deep in his throat. "I love when you say my name like that." His voice tugs at my insides, flutters through my very bones.

"I don't hate magic, I just…" But more kisses move down my throat, and my words trail off, because while I might hate that magic didn't save me—*I love how magic feels.*

I cling to him as his hot breath skates over my skin. "You do hate magic, and yet you're letting a faerie prince do this."

A prince? But—

His tongue takes the place of his kisses, pushing the thought away.

The alley spins, dark and cold, and filled with Cian.

His touch, his heat, his ragged breaths.

My skin pebbling.

"Are you really—" My words are cut off as his mouth comes dangerously close to mine. His breath feathers my lips, and my lungs restrict. His thumb rubs my bottom lip, and my sense leaves me completely. I no longer care about the risk of deadly obsession, I *need* to taste him. Now.

I lean forward, part my lips, and—

He steps away.

The magic bubble bursts, and all that remains is Cian, saying my name with no heat in his voice. "Saoirse."

Shit.

He drops his hands from my hips, and suddenly the night air is freezing against my damp skin. I pull my shirt sleeve back up over my shoulder, and try not to remember every move his lips and teeth, I gulp—his *tongue*, made across it.

Thankfully, the darkness hides the look in his eyes, but I feel his disappointment as keenly as if he's carved it into my bones. I sense more than see his jaw clench. "What were you thinking?"

I swallow. He knows I wasn't. And how could I be with the way he teased me? How did our moment of passion turn sour so quickly?

Then the thought of another man springs to my mind—Ask.

I should focus on repairing my relationship with the man I *want* to marry, not let Cian's hands wander all over me. Bile rises in my throat, and I squeeze my eyes closed.

When I open my eyes again, Cian is gone.

I stay outside for much too long, hoping the chilled night air will cool the embarrassment in my cheeks. It's about as effective as believing in magic.

Magic that couldn't save me then, and won't now.

Magic that makes me reckless with my life.

Magic I need to stay far, far away from.

CHAPTER 15

As the flint scrapes against the steel, a flame bursts forth under my hands.

The glowing lamp chases the shadows into the corners of my room. If only it could chase the ones in my mind as easily. Instead, the events of last night spin in my brain——around and around until I feel dizzy.

The sickening bruise on Finn's cheek. Cian's thunderous expression. His response to my horror. The stupid way I reacted to his thumb caressing my lower lip.

What if he hadn't stepped away? Would I be on my way to fatal obsession?

I've just laced up my dress waist when Cian appears in my room. My heart thunders in my chest, and I squelch a screech. What is he doing here? He can't just pop into my bedroom like this! What if I hadn't been dressed?

My cheeks grow hot at the thought.

But then I get a better look at him. His skin looks pale even in the yellow light, and dark shadows underline his beautiful eyes. Did he sleep at all? Or did he lie awake for the same reason I did?

I open my mouth to apologize for my foolishness last night, but before I can speak, he does.

"I made a mistake." His voice is flat.

My heart sinks. Of course, he thinks it was a mistake. I'm just a human, why would he actually want me? And why does the tightness in my chest feel so much like disappointment?

But then his voice cracks. "I shifted in front of Finn's uncle."

Cold settles in my stomach, and it takes effort to speak. "What?" The word is barely a breath.

He runs a hand over his face and muffles another curse. "He sprang at him. Right in front of me, and I couldn't just watch." His fingers push through his hair as he paces the tiny floorspace in my room, and I've never seen him this upset.

But then a thought strikes terror into my soul. Why is he here alone? Why isn't Finn with him?

Fear thins my blood, my laced waist suddenly too tight around my ribs, and I struggle to pull in a single breath. "Is Finn all right?"

I can't even look at him for fear of what he'll say.

But I can't *not* look at him.

And when I do, he pauses his pacing. "Finn is safe. For now."

His words unwind the terror-laced threads inside me, and my shoulders sink. But only for a moment—because if Finn is safe, why does Cian seem to be falling apart? "Did you... *hurt* him? Finn's uncle, I mean?"

He shakes his head. "I just knocked him out, but it doesn't matter."

I search his face, heartsore at the sorrow I see etched there. But if he didn't hurt Finn's uncle, there's no harm done, right? "I don't understand why you're so upset."

His green eyes drill into me, and in their depths is a sea of heartache. "I *can't go* to Finn anymore after this. He knows what I am, that I'm not just a cat. His uncle was drunk off his arse and might chalk it up to that, but Finn won't."

I still don't understand why he's grinding down the floorboards in my room like a caged bear. "Why can Finn not know what you are?"

He stops and pins me with a glare. "Because if he finds out *what* I am, he might find out *who* I am."

Breath stills in my lungs. "And *who* are you?"

His lips press shut.

He's not going to answer me. Just like every other time I've tried to ask about Finn's significance to this faerie whose people don't care about humans.

But then, he pulls in a deep breath and surprises me. The glassy sheen of tears turn his eyes an even darker green. "Finn… is my brother."

The air stills, and I don't think I'm breathing anymore.

His brother.

"Finn is a faerie?"

Cian shakes his head. "No. Finn is the son of my mother's second husband. Her human husband from the Northwoods."

"But humans can't kiss faeries? How—"

He cuts me off. "Marriage vows are sacred and render faerie magic useless. You know the stories."

I do know the stories—of ringing church bells breaking open the mountain to save human men from faerie captivity. Of the stavechurch keeping magic folk at bay and the humans inside them safe from their tricks.

But the stories don't hold my attention in the light of his earlier words. The ones I can barely comprehend as I drop down on the bed.

The frame creaks under my weight.

Finn is Cian's brother. His brother.

That is why he makes himself sick to stay with him overnight.

I look back up at Cian. "But why can he not know what you are?"

He shakes his head. "How would you feel if you were in his shoes, and you found out you had an older brother?"

I don't follow. I have been in Finn's shoes, or close to it—foisted upon a relative who never wanted the responsibility of a child. "I'd be elated that I had a brother and wasn't alone."

But Cian's eyes are sorrowful, the shadows in the room swirling with the grief in their depths. When he speaks, his voice is weak, defeated.

"And then what? When you found out your brother was a powerful prince in another country but still couldn't even take you away from the hell you were living?"

And I know this answer.

My heart shrinks in on itself, bleeding for both of them. "Devastated."

He dips his head.

Quiet fills my bedroom as his dark eyes trail my features. I don't know what to say. There are no words to ease his pain or Finn's.

The mere second his gaze rests on my lips is all it takes to heat my blood, but he looks away just as quickly. Clearly he's as loath to remember our heated moment as I am.

Why did I try to kiss him yesterday? *You're such a fool, Saoirse. He's trying to protect his brother, and you're trying to get yourself killed.*

I rise and step back from his magnetic presence, hoping physical distance will keep me safe from another reckless attempt to kiss him. "Why are you here?"

It's not like I can undo what happened at Finn's house. I'm certain he's not here just to talk. His swallow is audible in my quiet room. "I came to ask you to go in my stead."

I laugh. But when his serious expression doesn't waver, I clear my throat and run a hand down my scratchy wool skirts. "You've... already forgotten that I can't shift into a cat at will like you can? I'm not magical."

He shakes his head. "But you could be. I could make you."

I haven't had as much as a cup of coffee since I woke up, and the turn this conversation has taken is making me dizzy. Why on earth would I want him to do that? "I don't want to be magical."

He scoffs, runs his hand through his hair until it stands even more on end. He looks half-feral in the lamplight. "I'm plenty aware of your dislike of magical people, human, and I wouldn't ask for me. But I am asking for my brother."

I know what the faerie's presence means to Finn. I remember the terror in his voice both times when he thought his cat had died. But what Cian is asking is too much.

He wants to make me magical. And while I don't want that, would never in a hundred years want that, my *no* sticks in my throat.

Magic folk cannot be bargained with, nor be trusted.

I know I shouldn't bargain with a faerie, so why can't I tell him no? Because of his magic? Am I just too weak to withstand it?

I close my eyes. But if anything the draw towards him is even stronger in the dark behind my eyelids, and I open them as quickly. "There isn't another way? Why can't you just take him with you to Faerie?"

He stares at me as if *I'm* the one spouting preposterous ideas. "I can't just steal a human child. That's illegal."

My eyes widen. "Faeries have laws now?"

He snorts. "Of course we have laws."

A frown pulls at my brows. "Why would that be obvious to me? In all the stories I've ever heard, faeries do whatever they please, without consideration for the humans whose paths they cross."

Cian tips his head to the ceiling with a groan as if my reaction is unwarranted. Then his eyes flash to mine. "Did it ever occur to you that your grandmother's stories were just that —stories?"

I roll my eyes. "Yeah, until I met you."

His hands find his hips, and I don't want to admit how jaw-droppingly handsome he looks in the flickering lamplight.

He must catch my admiring gaze, because the corner of his lips tip up a little. A roguish smirk dances in his eyes. "Is that why you won't trust me? Because of an old woman's stories?"

I want to deny it, but it's true, isn't it?

I nod.

"What if she was wrong? What if those stories were told to foster a fear of what's foreign, to keep humans from exploring the world around them. Have you thought of that?"

"I have thought of that. But why would I assume my grandmother lied to me?" And if she did lie to keep me safe, can I hold it against her?

He shakes his head, and a dark laugh slips over his lips. "You haven't even asked me what you'd need to do for me to change you."

I shrug. I'm not considering it, so why would I ask for specifics? For a second my imagination runs wild—foul-tasting potions and blood-oaths, being locked into the mountain for the rest of my days, all trades for magical abilities in my grandmother's faerie tales. "What would I have to do?"

The expression in his eyes is somewhere between a taunt and a plea. "It involves that kiss you want so desperately. One that won't harm you."

My cheeks burn, and I swallow down the flutter in my chest. Kissing him doesn't feel like a chore, not if I can somehow circumvent the deadly obsession. "That's it? Only a kiss?"

He hesitates, and his eyes dip to his boots for a second before they light on mine. "No. Not only a kiss."

Never trust the faeries, Saoirse, they know no other way than deceit. He clears his throat, and I brace for what's coming.

But I'm still not ready when he speaks, his voice low and husky.

"You'd need to marry me."

CHAPTER 16

His words fill every crevice of space, and the world tilts. I must have slept more fitfully last night than I thought. Surely he didn't just suggest we get married?

I clear my throat. "I think I misheard you."

Cian slashes the air with his hand, his shirtsleeve a white flash in the dim light. The gesture might be angry, but I sense the hurt in his stiff shoulders. "Forget it. I knew you wouldn't. I'll find another way to save him." His harsh voice sounds one moment, and in the next he's gone.

And I'm alone.

The lamp sends flickers of yellow light over the darkened timber of walls and ceiling. The weird staccato rhythm of my heart blends with my frantic thoughts.

A faerie just asked me to marry him.

My grandmother warned me about this.

The most infuriating person, man or faerie, I've ever met just asked me to marry him. Not because he loves me, or even wants me. Only because he wants to save his brother from the crushing weight of being alone in the world.

As much as I haven't forgotten that feeling, I'm supposed to marry Ask. Need to marry Ask.

I can't marry Cian. I'm not even considering it. Why would I, when Ask is my key to a future without the uncertainty I knew as a child?

The uncertainty Finn is living now.

I finish dressing while Cian's words from earlier echo through my brain.

"He sprang at him. Right in front of me, and I couldn't just watch."

I suck in a breath. Where is Finn now? Is his uncle still knocked out? What might he do to him when he wakes up?

Suddenly every memory of my aunt's abuse crashes in over me.

Her throwing my favorite hair ribbon into the hearth, leaving me to sob as I watched it curl and burn.

The curved mark her teeth left on my arm.

The heaviness in my heart as I wondered, more than once, how one could live with such pain and not die.

Each memory the weight of a thousand rocks as it grinds me into nothingness. Finn's uncle may not be my aunt, but who's to say he's better? The heavy burden burrows back down inside me, where it lives now. And I know I would do anything to keep Finn from living another moment in the reality I knew then.

Anything.

I stand up so quickly the world disappears into blackness. When my vision returns, I snuff out the lamp, and fumble for my jacket. I fasten the hooks and eyes in the dark, then I hike up my skirts and sprint down the stairs and through the cabin.

Waving off a bewildered Ingerid, I wrench the door open and shut it behind me just as quickly. The late morning darkness wraps me like a cloak as I stomp down the steps through fresh snow creaking under my boots.

Soon, I'm in the alley, by the door where I've seen Cian sneak out so many times.

I knock softly, the wood cold against my bare knuckles. But the cabin is quiet, and no lights are visible from where I stand. Is his uncle still out cold? What will I do if he wakes up while I'm there? What will Finn do?

I pull deep, finding courage I didn't know I had. Then I open the door. It groans loudly, and I freeze. Blood pounds in my ears, but no sounds come from inside the cabin.

I step inside and feel my way through the dark interior, pausing every few steps to listen. With slow, halting steps, I make it all the way to the door at the top of the stairs, my heart thundering as if I've run the whole way.

I place my palm against the wood, force it open, and peer through the crack—steeling my heart for what I'll see.

Finn is curled up on his bed, backed as close against the wall as he can get. His head is buried into his knees, arms wrapped tightly around his legs. Even from here, I can see the tremble in his limbs.

I glance to where his uncle is stretched out on the floor, a purple bruise spreading over his jaw from where Cian must have decked him.

I clench my teeth. If I wasn't here for Finn, I'd give him a good kick myself.

Rather than exact my vengeance, I push the door open as far as it can go without hitting the man, step over his legs, and move towards the bed.

Finn looks up just as I get there, and his eyes well with tears. Leaning forward, I hold out my arms the way I would to a much smaller child. I pick him up and hold him close. He presses his body into my embrace, and everything inside me aches.

I carry him down the stairs. His breath is ragged, as if he, too, has been fleeing. As if he's still on the run.

Halfway down, I stop. "I need you to walk, love."

He slips down until his feet are on the steps, but his hand still white knuckles mine as I lead him through the dark cabin.

The door creaks into the night, startling us both. But then we cross the alley. Away away away.

I feel Cian's eyes on me from the darkened hollow and look up. But his gaze meets mine for only a second before he disappears into thin air.

I hurry inside the cabin, painfully aware of Finn's small hand tucked into mine. Ingerid is still crouched by the hearth. She looks from Finn to me, and opens her mouth, but I speak first. "Can you give Finn my portion of porridge, please? I don't think he's eaten yet."

She nods with her eyes full of questions.

I bring Finn over to the long bench and kneel on the floor next to him. "Ingerid will get you breakfast, and Liisa will walk you to the Pedersen farm after, all right?"

He nods, but as he blinks, his eyes turn shiny again. "My cat is gone. It attacked Master Johannes."

I nod and wrap both his cold hands in mine. "I know, and I'm so sorry. But he's safe, I promise."

While Finn pushes his porridge around the bowl with his wooden spoon, I pull Ingerid aside to tell her a brief version of the story—one that doesn't involve any magical people, or a marriage proposal. Liisa comes downstairs, ready to leave, and Ingerid pulls her aside, too.

I kneel next to Finn again, hoping desperately that the promises I make are not more than I can keep. "You can come back here with Liisa tonight and have your supper here."

He nods, but his eyes are doubtful. How I wish I could do more to ease his mind. Instead, I hug him tightly before he tucks his hand into Liisa's. From the doorway, I watch them walk down the hill, heart aching.

Then, I pull the last of my courage and walk through the star-studded darkness of a Northwoods morning.

Down to the hollow.

CHAPTER 17

On midsummer's day the year I turned eleven, I waded through the meadow behind my grandmother's cabin. I slipped my hand down the willowy flower stems and tugged, again and again, until I had twenty-three different kinds of wildflowers.

Full of girlish hopes, I tucked the bouquet under my pillow to dream about the man I'd marry—only to wake unable to recall the dream.

My grandmother had done the same, and I can still see her eyes shining at me from across the breakfast table the morning after.

"Did you dream of your one true love, Saoirse?"

My lips turn down as I pour the fresh cream over my porridge. "I don't know, I can't remember my dream. Did you?"

She smiles into her coffee. "Oh, yes." And it's like her youth is captured in that giggle—all the love she once knew shimmering in the warmth of her words.

I look up, hand paused halfway to my mouth and let the cream dribble from the lumpy porridge on the spoon. "Grandfather?"

Her eyes sparkle, and she tells my favorite story again.

Did I dream of Cian that night? My fists curl into my skirts as I fight the desire to turn and run, back inside our cabin where I'll be safe from this ridiculous notion.

But I can't shake the memory of Finn's arms clamped around my neck.

And I can't not go along with Cian's plan.

I groan and halt my steps again.

Because how can I agree to this marriage when I know what magic does to me? I can't help wanting it, the desire for the magic I longed for as a child is as strong as ever. But just last night, I almost kissed a faerie, even knowing what that kiss could do to me.

If magic makes that reckless, what might happen once it's within me? A shiver runs down my spine as the snow creaks softly under my boots.

I've spent the last week and a half with Ingerid, hemming and embroidering the linens she'll need for the home she'll make with Erkki, but I have nothing to bring to this marriage. And I've never seen Cian with more than the clothes on his back. But then, if I do this, it won't be a regular marriage, will it?

I'm in the hollow now. I pull in a breath of night air for the courage I don't possess, and step in under the canopy of sleepy, snow draped branches.

"Cian." I speak his name softly into the cold air.

We're still hours from sunrise, and the air seems even colder between the trees down here. It feels almost exactly like the first morning I saw him.

Except, I didn't follow a cat this time—I followed a desperate dream that I could make a difference.

I don't want magic, shouldn't want it.

What I do want is the safe home I didn't get to keep as a child. And I can have it if I only repair my relationship with Ask. He's the man I *should* marry. He'll make me happy enough, and more importantly—he'll keep me safe.

But how can I put my own comfort over the well-being of a child? Doesn't that make me just like my aunt? If I can protect Finn from the crushing loneliness still in my bones so many years later, won't even magic be worth it? Won't giving up Ask?

"Why are you here?" Cian's voice is as dark as the morning around us, and I startle. I'll never get used to the way he can appear from nowhere.

I try not to take offense at his prickly mood. "Because I want to help Finn."

"No." The angry word slices the air.

"Excuse me?" I take a step away from him. Did I misunderstand him earlier in my bedroom, or did he change his mind?

"I don't want to marry you." He grinds the words out.

I roll my eyes and pretend nothing shatters inside me at his dismissal. "You and your sweet talk." Every last one of my grandmother's stories warned me about how fickle faeries can be—perhaps I should have thought of that before I took this one's words for truth. "I guess we have nothing to talk about then."

I turn to leave, and walk straight into Cian's chest.

Damn faeries and their tricks!

I step back, but not far enough—I can still feel the heat from his body. "What are you doing?"

His gaze is so intent on mine I want to shrink back. "You would really do that? Marry me for Finn?"

Tears burn behind my eyes. He just rejected me in the rudest way possible and *now* he wants to talk? I blink the treacherous tears away and speak to his chest. "Yes, I would. Can I leave now?"

I don't have it in me to push him away. I don't want to touch his stupidly hard chest, or risk his nearness toying with my desire again.

I wait for him to move, but he doesn't. He just stands there like an immovable wall of everything I can't have and don't want.

You don't want him, Saoirse. You want safety, remember?

Ask's rugged features may never be as attractive as Cian's, and perhaps the flutters I feel with him are nowhere near as strong. But the safety he has to offer is worth more.

And I almost threw it away.

The thought makes me cold all over. But there's still time for me and Ask, as soon as this faerie moves to let me pass. "You are in my way. Please move so I can go about my day." I push the words out through gritted teeth, as if speaking them hurts me. And it does.

"You don't want to get married right now?"

I look up at him in disbelief. Is he toying with me again? But a frown mars his perfect brow, and my eyes go wide. "You just told me you didn't want to."

"As did you." He still makes no attempt to move.

I huff and fold my arms over my chest. If only that would protect my heart from his rapid mood changes. "You didn't even give me a chance to tell you why I came out here. I was going to tell you I would do it, and you told me to get lost."

He shrugs, looking nowhere near as repentant as the situation calls for. "I was upset about earlier."

I roll my eyes. Is he for real? "How very mature of you."

His full lips tilt a little, and I can't help but let my gaze trace the curve. He makes a throaty sound, and I flick my eyes upward to meet his unnerving gaze again. His eyes are the darkest green, like aged spruce needles and drenched moss.

I want to drown in them.

And that realization makes fear clog my throat.

My grandmother's warnings echo through my mind, my bones.

Faeries are evil.

Don't listen to them.

Beware.

Definitely don't go off and marry them.

But the warnings fade as I remember the bruise still visible on Finn's cheek this morning. I swallow and push the warmth in Ask's brown eyes from my mind.

I can do this for Finn. "Does it hurt?"

He lets out a surprised chuckle—the sound is so light, so warm, a tremble dances across my skin. "Marrying me? No. Do human marriages hurt?"

I think for a second. "I… wouldn't know. I've never tried. I don't think so?"

His lips tug, and I wonder if I can possibly get away unscathed from the smirk that blooms on his full lips. Sparkling green eyes hold mine until my breath hitches.

No. I might be many things by the end of this day, married even, but unscathed won't be one of them.

I tear my eyes away from his and study my hands.

This is madness. I want Ask to be my husband, not this faerie bound to change his mind about me again. I want to be the wife of a man strong enough to protect me, one kind enough to never use his strength to hurt me, or the children I give him.

But Finn?

Finn deserves what I never had.

I wet my lips. "So, what do I do?"

"You," he swallows, and his voice thickens a bit on his next words, "simply repeat the vows after me, and… seal it with a kiss."

My heart jolts in my chest, staggering into a staccato rhythm that makes me dizzy. I'll have to kiss him. *Do I want to kiss him?*

I tilt my head to look at him again, and hate the way my cheeks burn. "And your kiss won't hurt me, even though you don't love me?"

He stills, and his Adam's apple bobs quickly. But then the

frown on his forehead eases, and he shakes his head. "My kiss can't hurt you once we've spoken our vows."

"Are you sure?"

He nods, and I have to take his word for it. *Never trust the faeries.*

How can I even consider giving up the dream I've fostered for half of my life? The safe home I've longed for since I was a girl? And for what? "Are you actually a faerie prince?"

He nods. "Does that change your mind?"

I shake my head. Why would it? "It wouldn't make a difference to me if you were a faerie beggar."

He huffs. "Your flattery could use some work."

But I won't take the bait. *Can't* take the bait. Not with my throat thickening and my mouth going dry. I swallow one last time, and make a decision I'm certain I'll regret. "Let's do it."

He clears his throat, and holds out his hands. I stare at them as if they might bite me. And who knows? Maybe they will. "Saoirse, I need your hands."

I place my hands in his and try not to tremble at the pulse of magic under his skin, at the warmth coloring the inside of my chest. *At this madness.*

"I also need you to breathe, so you don't pass out." A small laugh slips over his lips.

Oh, right. Breathing is good. I pull in a deep breath.

He crosses our hands and switches his grip from one to the other. How are his hands so warm in this cold?

A thick, silver ribbon appears as if by magic, circling our hands. The swirl of cool fabric tightens against my skin, and Cian speaks vows I've heard at every wedding I've attended at the stave church. But they sound different in this hollow. So very different when I'm about to tie my life to his.

Cian's eyes don't move from my lips as I repeat his vows. He holds unnervingly still, as if his life depends on each syllable trickling from my mouth. "All the days of my life."

Life.

I close my mouth over that last word, and wet suddenly parched lips.

Then, Cian leans down to close his lips over mine.

And the world.

Stops.

His mouth is so soft, so warm, so—

He pulls back almost immediately, and I'm frozen in the gravity of what I've just done.

I've married a faerie.

Bile rises in my throat. My head is too light, and spots dance in my vision.

A cloud descends on Cian's furrowed brow. *My husband's furrowed brow.*

I'm going to pass out.

"Saoirse, relax." Cian's thumbs caress my cheeks, and he tilts my head until my eyes meet his. My breaths are too shallow, my skin prickling as it goes numb under his hands. My words rasps through a throat as dry as paper. "Am I magical now?"

"Yes." His voice wraps around me, breathes life back into my skin, calms my racing heart. As my breaths even, he leans forward, a question in his eyes.

One I'm fairly certain has all wrong answers. A *yes* goes against every warning my grandmother ever spoke. A *no* makes me shudder at what I would be missing.

I dip my chin. *I've sold my future to the magic folk, I might as well go all in.*

And then, Cian kisses me again, and I understand why faerie kisses lead to deadly obsession.

Because his mouth tastes like a spring morning.

Like that sacred moment of a sunrise when color and light descends on earth.

His skin is warmth and brightness, and his every touch—on my neck, my arms, my face—burns through my skin until his hands press against my bare soul. Until nothing I ever do will wash away his fingerprints.

When he pulls back, cold darkness descends on us. "That didn't hurt, did it?" His voice is hoarse, his breath racing past his lips as fast as mine.

I shake my head. "You taste like magic." My breathless voice sounds nothing like my own, but my words make the light dance in his eyes.

He pulls me close again, and his hot breath whispers over my lips. "Because I am."

CHAPTER 18

The snowy landscape is pink from an afternoon sunset, and my lips still tingle from Cian's magical kiss. Nighttime will be here in a few hours, and once it is, I will shift into a cat to stay with Finn. I don't even know the process involved, and already my stomach is curdled with nerves.

I pace the main room until I glimpse two dark figures through the bubbly window panes. The door creaks open as Liisa coerces a reluctant Finn inside.

"Master Johannes will expect me home." Finn's voice shakes, and I have some choice names I'd like to call Master Johannes for that. But instead, I take Finn's hand and lead him to the bench. Ingerid puts down her mending and pours steaming mutton and cabbage stew into a bowl. The delicious aroma wafting up from it makes my mouth water.

While Finn slurps hot broth, Ingerid pulls me aside. "Do we really have to send him back next door?"

I close my eyes and wish my answer could be different. "I'm afraid so. Master Johannes must have regained his faculties by now, and Finn's not ours to keep."

Nor is he mine, as much as I desperately wish he was.

Ingerid sighs, and her eyes look a little glassy as she glances over at the little boy. And even though I know Finn won't have to be alone tonight, I push down a sigh equally deep. I can't tell either Ingerid or Finn that I plan to keep him company as a cat.

And I'm not even sure exactly how it will help.

I chew on my thumb. Just the thought of shifting makes nausea burn in my throat. Cian didn't mention any particulars this morning, and I haven't seen him since. Our exchange of vows and his kiss, while nice, didn't exactly enlighten me.

I don't feel any more magical than I did before, so I'm just going to have to take Cian's word for it. *Trusting a faerie. Such a bright plan, Saoirse.*

When Finn finishes his supper, I have no choice but to walk him across the alley between our cabins. "Would you like me to come in with you?" I have no wish to lay eyes on Master Johannes ever again, but if I can smooth over any upset he feels so that Finn doesn't take the brunt of it, I will. "I can talk to him and explain where you've been."

But Finn shakes his head. I watch him walk through the door with the air of a soldier going off to war, and my heart bleeds.

He won't ask for my help, even if he needs it, and the very thought breaks my heart. *Please ask, Finn.*

"You care for him."

I spin around, heart galloping wildly in my chest. I recognize Cian's stance in the shadows by the tar-darkened wall, and a relieved breath leaves me. "Of course, I do. Why do you think I agreed to marry you?"

The words come out sharper than I intend, but he just scared a year off my life. He flinches, but doesn't refute my words. He knows as well as I that they are true—I never would have married him if not to help Finn.

Ask's lopsided smile as he pulled me close that night at the tavern slides into my mind's eye. But the memory carries a sting now, so I push it away.

I made my choice. However stupid a choice it might have been.

I clear my throat. "You never told me how I'd shift into a cat."

"I didn't?" He knows he didn't. It's not like I'd forget. "Why don't you come over here, and I'll tell you." Something in his voice makes me hesitate. Whatever it is, it's more commanding, more frightening, than anything I've heard in it before.

I swallow and try to keep my frantic thoughts at bay—but they come anyway, thrashing wildly inside my skull. *I have a faerie for a husband, and I have no idea what he expects of me. Do not trust the faeries.*

I step closer, and he tilts his head to look down at me. The faint light catches his glittering eyes, and goosebumps break out on my skin.

Get a grip, Saoirse! He hasn't even touched you.

But do I want him to? *Should* I want him to?

The attraction I feel, have felt since we met, is nothing but the natural way faeries affect humans. It doesn't mean anything.

I can't read his expression in the dark, but I'm infinitely aware of the air that tingles between us. Like frost on a winter's morning, I know it will bite at first—then melt under my touch. Will his touch be the same? Do I want it to?

Yes.

He chuckles darkly, as if he can hear my spinning thoughts. Then he leans forward until our mouths are only a breath apart. "Do you have a kiss for your husband?"

His voice is smooth and warm, slithering under my skin and heating my blood. I squirm under his intense gaze, my voice barely a breath. "Your kiss won't hurt me?"

He smirks, and his teeth, white in the dark, grace his bottom lip. "Not unless you want it to."

I push out a surprised breath, and my face grows hot.

Then his lips are on mine, and I lose my grip on any coherent thought. His kiss, his touch—there's no other way to describe it other than magic.

I moan into his mouth, and his clamps around my back, crushing me to his chest. My head spins, and my spine floats. And as Cian's kiss explodes through my veins like sunbursts through winter woods, I can't deny the magic between us.

Ask has never set my blood on fire like this.

When he finally wrenches free from my lips, we're both breathing hard. I tremble as the frozen air cools every place his body pressed against mine.

What was that? And why do I want it again?

I only married him so I could give Finn a semblance of safety. That is what I should be concerned about. Not Cian's kisses, or his anything else.

My skin heats, and I push that thought away. "Will you teach me to shift now?"

"Not here." His breath is still labored, and part of me is very happy he's as affected as I am.

"I'll meet you in your room." He nods to the cabin, and I try to gather my liquefied limbs to convince them to move. They eventually comply.

Inside, Ingerid knits furiously on a pair of mittens by the hearth, her brow furrowed in concentration. I step over a ball of blue yarn and another the color of mustard. She looks up. "Where are you going?"

I halt as guilt prods my heart, as if she's caught me sneaking the last of the mulled wine. But I haven't. I've done something far worse. *I've married a faerie, and I'm keeping it from her.* "I need to go to bed, my headache is getting worse."

Ingerid's gaze drifts over me. "You don't look too good. But your headaches are just going to get worse the way you keep running outside in nothing but your shirtsleeves, Saoirse."

I grimace, and nod. "I'll try not to."

Liisa sits closer to the fire, yards of fabric draped across her lap. But she doesn't even look up, and I push down the twinge of hurt. As much as I want to drop to my knees and beg her forgiveness, I don't think it would heal the rift between us.

And right now, I need to get upstairs.

To wait for my faerie husband.

I shudder, fold my arms across my chest to stave off the goosebumps, and move slowly up the stairs.

I've barely shut the door when he appears.

My heart jumps into my throat, because we're married, in my room, and I have no idea what he expects. And after the wild kisses outside, my mind and body is at war about what we *want* to happen. I move to light the lamp, but he shakes his head.

He watches me quietly for a moment. "You want me to teach you to shift?" There is a challenge in his voice I don't understand.

Why is he so hesitant to show me? "That's why we're here, isn't it?" He nods. I wait and try not to squirm under his scrutiny. "So, what do I do?"

He pulls in a deep breath. "It's hard to explain. Here, let me show you." He steps so close to me our bodies touch from hips to neck. All of him pressed up against me like this, does things to me that I find hard to ignore.

He clears his throat. "Touch me."

"What?" I croak the word out.

"Just do it." He grabs my hand and places it over his heart, and relief trickles through me. "I'm going to shift, and I need you to keep your hand on me while I'm doing it."

I nod and relax the hand pressed against his chest.

Do faeries have hearts like humans do? From the increasing rhythm under my fingers, it seems likely. And then, his chest warms until my palm burns.

"Don't let go. The magic won't hurt you." His voice sounds strange, as if it's coming from further away, even though he's still right here. I close my eyes a second before the flash comes, and my knees bend as he shrinks to the floor.

I don't know what he's doing, but the magic moves through my hand, into my arm. It trickles from my shoulder down into my chest, and I still wouldn't be able to put it into words. But I know what I must do.

"Should I do it now?" I look at the fully formed tabby cat in front of me, whose green eyes watch me intently. Its head dips, and embarrassment warms my face.

Why did I expect a cat to speak?

I keep my hand pressed to the tabby's silky chest as I hold its eyes. Cian's eyes.

And then, I shift.

Fear snarls around my throat as my skin warms and tightens. My bones shift and the sensation makes nausea swirl at the back of my throat.

It doesn't hurt, I don't think, but it's not at all comfortable.

I can't do this, I need to stop it. Why did I think I could do this?

Never trust the faeries.

But in another moment, my vision sharpens, and I see purple flecks in Cian's eyes I've never seen before. Eyes that are parallel with mine even as I stand upright—on four legs.

Fear closes around my heart as this realization pummels through me.

I am no longer human.

CHAPTER 19

I push my head against the door of Finn's cabin.

It creaks open, and a second later, I'm inside. The mucky floor boards smell even ranker this close to my nose. I tap soundlessly up the stairs on soft paws. Loud snores come from the first room, and I shudder as I move past. Then I trip nervously into Finn's room. He gasps as he sees me. "Did my cat send you?"

Am I supposed to answer that? Would Cian? I dip my head and hope it isn't the wrong thing to do. But Finn's relieved smile makes me think I chose right. He pats his bed, and I jump to curl up on the mattress edge, next to his pillow. *Is this what I'm supposed to do? What Cian did?*

But then, Finn's small, warm arm snakes around me. Softly, he strokes the fur on my back, his whisper so quiet it would barely be audible to human ears. "I'm so glad you're here."

I WOBBLE down the stairs in the morning hours, my feline stealth all but gone from exhaustion. Master Johannes's snores reverberate through the cabin, and I can still hear Finn's even breaths upstairs in his room from a floor below. By the time I push through to the outside, I'm ready to collapse.

Out of habit, I glance towards the hollow. And not in a hundred years do I expect to see the ethereally beautiful woman standing next to my husband.

Pain crashes into my chest. Bile rises in my throat, and I can't keep down last night's dinner any more than I can push the hurt away.

Why does the sight of them together hurt so much?

I dry-heave as my bones elongate and my skin stretches. It hurts. It hurts so badly. If I wasn't too exhausted, I would scream. I sob quietly as my forehead rests on the cold stone step.

Heavy boot steps approach, but I can't seem to move, even though I should. Whoever it is might have seen me shift, and if they did, I don't even know what would happen to me.

People in the Northwoods might tell the stories of magic, but in their tales too, magic is evil.

"Shit. Saoirse." Strong arms wrap around me. The cold rock moves away from my forehead, and the world spins as my stockinged feet leave the frosty grass. I think I'm going to hurl again at the jostling movement. But my stomach is empty, and the spasms do nothing but hurt my already aching body.

A door creaks open, and concerned voices surround us, but we don't stop. I'm rocked again as heavy boots hit stair step after stair step.

My stomach aches with another dry heave, and I whimper.

"Are you in pain, my heart?" The velvety soft voice curls around my ribs like the softest caress, but who would call me that? As far as I know, my heart doesn't belong to anyone. I try to force the words to make sense through the painful fog in my brain, but they don't. "Ask?"

A rueful chuckle sounds too close to my brain, and I recognize Cian's voice. "Wrong man, love."

I did choose the wrong man, didn't I? I chose a magical faerie over a man who'd never spend any time with otherworldly women, or other women at all.

Cian carries me through a doorway, and in another moment I'm curled in a heap on a soft bed. My own, I'm fairly sure.

A warm cloth wipes at my quivering chin, my cracked lips, down my throat. "Can I help you out of your dress? You're covered in puke." His words should make me feel embarrassed, but I can't find it in me to care.

I nod, instantly regretting the move as nausea twirls back up my throat. Strong fingers unlace my waist front with expert movements. In another moment, he's unhooked my skirt and belt, and helped me shrug out of the waist.

I'm left only in the white linen shirt that barely covers my backside.

With Cian, who I'm married to.

In my bedroom.

If I wasn't so sick, I'd have thoughts about this. *A lot of thoughts.*

But Cian makes no reference to our vows as he helps me crawl under the covers. Forever seems to pass, and he still hasn't left. But he also hasn't made any attempts to get into my bed.

Another wave of pain pushes through my body, and I grit my teeth. "Does it always hurt like this?"

His sigh is deep. "No, I should have prepared you better."

God, yes, he should have! "Are you leaving now?"

"Not unless you want me to." His voice is close enough he must be kneeling by my bed, but that can't be right.

"Don't you have company?" I hope he doesn't pick up on the

jealousy in my voice. I don't want to be jealous. I have no reason to be—ours isn't a love match.

He chuckles darkly. "She left, and she's no one to me, Saoirse."

He's a faerie, and I shouldn't take his word for anything, but his answer sends a trickle of relief through my veins. And suddenly I want him to stay. Badly.

Another shiver racks my body. "I'm so cold." He tugs another blanket up over me, but I need more. I push the words past my lips before I can talk myself out of them. "I want you."

His hand stills on my blanket for a full second as if he's holding his breath. "You want me?"

"To warm up." My teeth chatter. I know it's exhaustion, not cold. But I still can't think of anything more soothing than a warm body tucked under the covers with me. Even if that body has to be a faerie's. "Please."

Cian pulls his hand away and stands up.

He's going to leave. My heart jolts weakly in my chest—I don't want him to leave.

But then a heavy weight thuds against the floor, followed by another. If he's taking his boots off does it mean he'll stay?

The mattress dips, and Cian takes up most of the room in the bed—like he does the space in my head. He's so warm, and curled into him my shivers evaporate like a snowflake in the sunshine. Reveling in his closeness, I press my face to where his heart beats rapidly under his shirt. Is he as affected by my touch as I am by his?

"I know you've been told not to trust me." His warm breath dances over the crown of my head. "But I'll show you that you can."

Before I can respond, or even think what words to use, he whispers my name. And just like the first time he did so, I drift into a dreamless sleep.

CHAPTER 20

Warmth kisses my closed eyelids. Slowly, I open one eye, then immediately jam it shut to keep the punishing brightness out. My temples pound.

Am I sick? Is that why I'm still in bed? If the sun is this bright it must be past noon, at least. Like everyone else living this far north, I both wake and fall asleep to the velvety winter darkness. Waking with the sun is for summertime, not for the cold season.

I make a half-hearted attempt to move, to find Ingerid and Liisa and find out why they haven't woken me. But my limbs aren't ready to leave my warm cocoon. Even less so when the blankets tighten around me, and the fresh scent of spruce woods tickles my nose.

A rush of breath heats the back of my neck, and I freeze.

I'm not alone.

Cian is here. Cian, who is also my husband. That thought sends a thrill through me, and gooseflesh erupts across my neck, releasing a dark chuckle from the faerie behind me.

"Morning, wife." Cian's whisper is hot against my throat, and my body melts like a snowbank in the sun. "Liisa was just here to check on you."

My heart pounds, and it takes me a second to decipher his words. When I do, my heart sinks. "She... found us here together again?" I close my eyes on a groan. Now she'll really never forgive me.

Cian's slides his large hand up to rub my shoulder through my linen shirt. "I told her we're together." Together, not married.

My eyes flutter closed again as his fingers caress my collar bone, and I want to ignore his words. Why does his touch feel so all-consuming? Is it because of his faerie magic, or does it feel like this with humans, too?

But Liisa is the closest I'll ever be to having a younger sister, so I speak the inkling I've had for a while now. "I think... she has a crush on you."

He chuckles as if this doesn't bother him the way it does me. Or at all. "She'll be fine, love." That last word swirls through me, swiping at tissues and bones until it reaches the parts that can't be seen, only felt.

Love.

Cian married me, but he doesn't love me. Are faeries even able to love? Did I pass up my chance of safety with Ask for a life with a faerie that can't love me?

I might have.

But then I remember the relief in Finn's voice last night, and I can't regret my choice.

Besides, while my new husband might not love me, he's cared for me tenderly since I collapsed on the stone steps this morning. And even though I'm all but naked tucked into bed with him, he's done nothing to make me feel pressured. With or without love, Cian's lips give the dizzying red currant wine I had in the tavern a run for its money.

I've hated magic ever since the days following my grandmother's death. When I waited so desperately for the magic folk to show up and save me, and… they didn't.

But when Cian's mouth skims the spot below my ear, a sigh slips over my lips.

And the truth is that I don't hate this at all.

WHEN I WAKE AGAIN, I'm buried against Cian's warm shirt. I pull back far enough to catch the sparkle in his eyes that signifies that *he's* not just woken up. Did I fall asleep while he kissed my neck?

My cheeks warm, but my head no longer pounds, and the light behind the curtains is dim and warm. I yawn, stretch my neck, trying to work the kink out of my shoulders. "Do you have nothing better to do than staying in this bed with me?" His grin widens, and something stirs deep in my chest. Something I'm not brave enough to name.

"Good evening to you too." His warm breath precedes the lips he presses to my neck. "And no, I don't."

"You're a prince, right? Don't you have a kingdom to rule?"

He chuckles into my neck, and blood rushes through my body. "Yes, but I'll go back tonight once you shift."

Back. To Faerie, and… the woman I saw in the hollow? Surely she's a faerie too? I won't ask, but even as the thought slips through my mind my shoulders tense. I have a right to know, don't I?

The question slips over my lips before I can push it back down. "Who was the woman in the hollow?"

Cian's whole body stills before he lets out a warm breath against my neck, and my heart aches. It's a tired breath, full of frustration and… guilt?

Shards of betrayal slice at my heart.

Please let me be wrong, please let it not be guilt. I'm not a fool. I know I'm not Cian's wife for any other reason than his love for his brother, but please, let him at least be faithful still. We've only been married a day.

His swallow is audible. "She's my... advisor." *No. No. No.*

"But she's more than that, right? Or you wouldn't freeze when questioned about her?" My voice is small, cool, untouched by the agony I feel. Untouched by the warmth of his arms still around me.

He sighs, loosens his hold on me, and lets me go, shattering my heart just a little more with that one movement. He shakes his head. "No. She's not more to me now."

If not *now*, then when? Sadness trickles like ice down my back, chilling me to my core.

His fingertip traces my neck, tips up my chin until my gaze meets his. "A long time ago, when I was much younger, Saoirse. I would not break my vows to you."

I stare into his eyes, plunge into the mossy depths as best I can, but is that pure twinkle *truth*? Or just faerie magic? Surely some of the stories are true? Faeries wouldn't have such a shoddy reputation without there being a grain of truth to it, would they?

I shake my head. "It doesn't matter."

Darkness swirls in the depths of his eyes, his voice hot. "What? Why wouldn't it matter?"

I swallow the painful lump in my throat and shrug as nonchalantly as I can. "I can't stop you from going home with her, can I?"

His eyes turn stormy, and I amend my words. "Home to faerie. You told me you can't stay away for long without getting sick."

"That's while staying a cat. And even if that was true, it doesn't mean I'd break my word to you."

"Alright." But there's no conviction in my voice.

The magic folk know no other way than deceit.

And yet, I was the girl foolish enough to bind myself to one. But I can't change that now, and I wouldn't if I could. Saving Finn from the aching loneliness I knew as a child will have to be enough. It is enough.

I glance to the window where the red glow has dimmed. "Is it almost night time?"

He follows my gaze. "Yes."

Vivid memories assault my brain. Waking up in Finn's room with weakness surging through my bones. Losing my dinner on the stone steps outside his cabin. Cian carrying me, wiping my chin with cool cloths. Pulling my soiled clothes off me. I shudder. "Will I be this sick tomorrow, too?"

He swallows and brushes a finger down my face. His every touch makes my skin come alive. I should hate it, especially now that I know who he's with when he's away.

But I don't hate it. *Oh, how desperately I don't.*

He leans in and replaces his finger with his lips. "I don't think so. It should get easier the more you do it."

I sink into him, his touch, his mouth.

If I'm going to feel like death later, the least he can do is make it worth my time. And I'm going to enjoy this moment, this kiss, to the fullest.

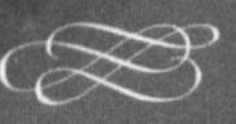

CHAPTER 21

I'm curled up in Finn's empty bed when I peel my eyes open. The room blurs as nausea clamps around my stomach as I push up from the wrinkled sheet.

Then the floor moves towards me at a dizzying speed. I land on the floorboards with a thump, in direct opposition to the feline grace I should possess.

My whole side aches as I creep down the stairs. Not a sliver of moon is visible in the velvet sky when I push the door open. Sensing movement in the hollow, I turn that way. My paws tap lightly against the icy top layer of the snow, and I hurry towards our meeting spot.

A breeze slips its frozen fingers around my small body, and I hunch my shoulders as I speed up. Finally, I'm hidden in the shadows of the trees.

I catch Cian's scent on the air before I see him. Spruce and midnight, tantalizing and comforting all at once. The night might be his domain. But spruce woods have surrounded me since the day I was born, and will till the day I die—and they are mine.

I will my body to shift, then groan as my insides twist to

turn human again. I sway on my feet, but Cian's arms wrap around me, and I stay upright.

Why, after just a day of this marriage does his arms around me feel so natural? Is this what I've been fighting since we met? The tension that's trickled through me whenever he's been around? Those butterflies in my middle that I could never muster in Ask's presence?

Cian's breath feathers my lips, and the nausea fades a bit as I tilt towards him. His lips are warm, and so, so soft. I moan when he pulls away.

"Do you know tonight is the longest, darkest night of the year?"

I shake my head. "I forgot."

He pulls me close, and his solid warmth staves off the winter chill all around us. He looks down at me, eyes dark as he takes me in. "Do you know what faeries do on this night?"

"What?" My voice is breathless in the half-dark.

His eyes sparkle, clearer than the stars above us. "We dance. What do humans do?"

I laugh, because my answer doesn't make us sound nearly as refined as the faeries. "Drink ale."

His eyebrows rise. "Really?"

I nod. "It's ale-tasting night, when we visit neighboring farms to taste the ale they've brewed for Yuletide."

"So you get drunk?" His laughing mouth finds mine again, moves down to my chin and lands a kiss there. "It sounds like those two traditions can be combined, don't you think?"

If I didn't before, his mouth has everything it takes to convince me.

We cling to each other as we stumble up through the alley. Cian fumbles blindly with the door latch without moving his mouth from mine. The cabin is empty, but even if it hadn't been, the way Cian's hands skim over my waist would have me indifferent.

We pause at the stairs, and Cian presses me up against the wall while planting sloppy kisses down my neck, over my face. He hoists me up into his arms and take the stairs in two steps.

I can't focus on anything but him. His arms around me. The dizzying sensation of his breath on my neck. His teeth nipping my collar bone.

I kiss his nose and laugh at the face he makes. Then he swallows my laughter and backs us through my bedroom door. And I can't say I'm displeased in any way.

WE DON'T MAKE it out of my room until Ingerid calls up the stairs. Long after the darkest night has fallen over the Northwoods. Yellow torchlight filters through the wavy window panes, and Cian's slips his hand around my waist halfway down the stairs. I turn my head for one more kiss.

Two more.

I stifle a yawn as I walk into the room with Cian hot on my heels.

Ingerid sends me a questioning glance. "You look... very tired for someone who slept away all the daylight."

Cian throws his head back and laughs, and my face burns at the implication his outburst all but confirms. Head lowered, I reach for my shawl and hope my voice doesn't betray my embarrassment. "Whose farm are we going to first?"

"The one next door." Liisa slips past me, already dressed. "Are we bringing these, Ingerid?"

Wrapped loaves are piled on the table, and I feel a stab of guilt. I should have helped Ingerid bake them earlier. Sure, I was exhausted from shifting, and the sleep I get in my cat body is nothing compared to sleeping as a human. But thanks to Cian, everyone knows sleep isn't what has taken up the most of my time today.

I dare a look at my stupid faerie husband, but his eyes are already on me, and the wicked grin he sends me does nothing to make the guilt go away.

"I made honey cakes." Ingerid scoops the wrapped loaves into her arms. She passes several to Cian, then turns to me. "Saoirse, will you drop these if I make you carry some?"

Flustered, I shake my head, but Ingerid's eyes are full of laughter. She knows exactly how embarrassed I am.

Liisa clutches her packages close to her blue wool cloak. Her gaze moves from my red face to Cian's smirk. "So if you two are together, what about Ask?"

Does she know how deeply that barb hits? Maybe.

But I deserve it either way.

"Ask and I haven't even... we're not anything." My words bite into the air, into my heart. Liisa may not know *why* I've pined for Ask, but she knows I have. In her eyes, I only showed interest in Cian after I saw her dancing with him.

Her dark eyes are narrowed, and I know I'll have questions to answer later.

Did I make a mistake when I chose Cian? But no, I couldn't have. Ensuring Finn's safety is a much nobler cause than my silly crush on a blacksmith's son, isn't it? *My silly crush on a safe future.*

I push the thought away, pull my mittens on, and grab the last several loaves from the table. Liisa, Ingerid, and Cian file behind me out through the door.

We step into a dark night filled with jingling horse harnesses, loud, happy voices, and laughter. Snow crunches under my boots, and the freezing air immediately wraps around my stocking-clad legs.

I step to the side to let the others pass and glance towards Finn's house. It's dark and quiet. Cian's arm wraps around my shoulder and tugs me into his hard chest. "You know we can't take him with us ale-tasting." His whisper is hot against my ear.

Breath leaves my lungs in a puff of white smoke, and I nod. All I want is to lean into Cian, let him wrap me up in his arms and hold me until all these worries cease. Instead, I pull in another breath of frosty winter air and steady my voice. "I know. But I just... what if he's alone?"

Cian lets out a deep breath. "Then he's probably happy to be free from his uncle's company for a bit."

I chew on my lip, but Cian is right. Finn would be happy to have respite for an evening. *I know I always was.*

Cian lets out a tsk-ing sound. "Oi, human, that's a surefire way to get your lips frostbit if I ever saw one." The note of mischief is back in his voice. It swirls around my core and warms me from the inside out.

I let my lip go and look up at him, eyes wide and innocent. "Who's going to bite them if I don't?"

His gaze darkens, and anticipation tightens my stomach. But instead of tipping his head down to kiss me, his eyes fill with a sparkle that rivals the starry sky above him. Then he throws his head back and laughs.

I should be disappointed, but I'm not.

I didn't know faeries could be like this—that Cian could be like this. That the warnings in my grandmother's stories were for the joy that springs up in me now.

He tugs me even closer, presses his lips to my forehead, and my eyes flutter closed.

"Hey you two, no kissing breaks. We're not even at the first farm yet." Liisa's voice is loud and clear in the cold air, and laughter erupts behind us at her words. My ears burn under my hood. How did Erkki and his friends get here already? They weren't here when we came outside, were they?

I turn away from Finn's cabin and step up into the snowy bank between us and the rest of our group. My leg immediately sinks in down to my knee.

"Here." Cian comes alongside me and reaches for my hand. His mittened one clamps around mine as he pulls me over the top of the drift and down to where the group is gathered.

There's no end to the hollers and whistles as the group zero in on the arm Cian slides around my waist as soon as I'm back on solid ground. I look for familiar faces and pretend my red cheeks are from the cold, not the entirely correct insinuations in their shouts.

Erkki's arm tightens around Ingerid's waist, and he smirks at me. But it's no secret that they're to be married soon—the banns have been read for them two Sundays in a row. Whereas for me and Cian there's been no such announcement.

I spot several girls I don't know, as well as Kari Bakken, who has never let a chance to make me look just a little worse slip by her. I'm sure tonight will be no different. As if she's read my thoughts, she tilts her head to whisper into her friend's ear. They both stare at me and laugh, and I groan inwardly.

Erkki takes the lead and soon his fist hammers on our neighbor's door. It creaks open, spilling golden light into the darkness around us.

"Good evening, welcome!" A red-cheeked woman glances over Erkki's head, eyes widening as she surveys the group. "Oh, you're quite a crowd out walking tonight, aren't you? Well, come in."

We go inside the smoky main house where a stove pumps out blessed heat to warm our already frozen hands and faces. Cian pulls me down next to him on the bench along the wall, and soon we're all seated. Hoods and hats are pulled off and snowy mittens removed. The Yuletide ale is passed around, but I can't take my eyes off the couple who lives here.

The woman's husband watches her with glittering eyes, and her cheeks flush as she catches his gaze. She's no beauty, but as the crows' feet by her eyes deepen in a smile, it's hard to remember that. Her chapped hand smooths down her wrinkled linen apron as she pulls another jug of ale from the barrel and hands it to her husband.

They've been married for as long as I've been alive, I think, and still the love between them is so strong it's tangible. Magical.

Is that what magic really is?

I don't dare glance at the faerie next to me. I'd long ago decided to give up the stolen glances between my neighbors. I didn't want what they had more than I wanted the safety I had as a child. Not more than the freedom from cowering under an angry tirade.

Ask always liked me more than I liked him, I think, because to me he was just a means to an end. Not that it matters now. I've given up the safe home I could have had with him, too. So that Finn will have a semblance of peace.

Cian's kisses are sweet now, but he'll tire of me eventually. I'm just a human girl—I'll grow old, and without love, there won't be this.

No, I'll never have what they have, but watching them tonight is still a gift.

I close my eyes and try to hold on to the memory. I tell myself it's enough.

But then the stoneware jug makes its way to us, and my eyes flutter open. One sip, and the liquid glides cool and strong down my throat.

I hand the jar to Cian who tips it back and passes it to the man on his left. He bumps me with his elbow and sends me a smirk. "If it's this strong all night, I suspect I'll be carrying you home at the end of it."

Images of the way he carried me home from the tavern crowd into my mind, and my cheeks heat. Truth be told, I wouldn't mind him carrying me home. But then the image of me puking my guts out once he set me down pushes its way through my memories, and I wince. "If the sips are small enough, I'll be fine."

His eyes glitter, as if he has no faith in me keeping them small. "We'll, see, human, won't we." He whispers the last part into my ear, but I still jab him with my elbow.

"Don't!" My whisper is hot and angry against his ear, but how is he not afraid of people finding out what he is? Infuriating man. Faerie.

"You worry too much… *love.*"

My stomach flips at his endearment, and I gasp before I catch the laughter in his eyes. Of course he's only teasing. He doesn't love me. Won't ever love me.

"Alright, next house." Erkki again. There's a few murmurs of protest, but everyone stands, pull their mittens back on and adjust hoods, scarves, and hats. Then shouted thanks to our hosts and wishes for a merry Yuletide echo between the walls as we mill out the door.

"Thank you." I squeeze the woman's hand at the door, and my words are for more than sharing their ale. Then I step back into the longest, darkest night of the year, and stomp through the snow beside Cian.

Two hooded figures pass so closely their skirts brush mine. "You'd think she'd know better than to take such massive drinks from the jug." Kari's voice is just loud enough I can hear it clearly, and drips with disdain.

Her friend tucks back her hood with a mittened hand, and glances at me. She snorts. "What did you expect from an orphan?"

Kari laughs, a pearly laugh so fake it hurts my ears. "True." Her eyes narrow at me, and she walks off, skirts swaying.

I roll my eyes. Cian bends down to me. "Friends of yours?"

It's my turn to snort. "Not by a long shot."

"Want me to sort them out?" His voice is cooler than the air around us as he watches their dark silhouettes. I feel the magic swirl around him. I don't know how I can feel that, but I do.

I clamp my fingers down on his arm. "No! I don't want you to do anything!"

He huffs. "You're going to let them talk to you like that?"

I shrug, loosening my deathgrip only slightly. "They don't know me. I do. Their words don't matter."

He nods, then straightens. "I like that about you."

I push out a breath as my hand relaxes and drops from his arm. "Thank you."

The grin he sends me is devastating, and my heart tumbles in my chest. Why does he do that to me? What we have is attraction, nothing more. My heart needs to stay out of this.

After the third farm, we take a shortcut through the woods. Pushed to the side, snow laden branches send their burdens flying into the air—as well as into an unfortunate face or two. Screeches sound from the people with facefuls of snow, followed by barks of laughter from the ones in front who were supposed to hold the branches back.

But the scolding voices fade to the background as Cian steps in front of me to hold back a particularly snowy spruce branch. Mischief dances in his eyes, and I brace for a faceful of snow. But he doesn't let go.

I huff and bump into him a little harder than necessary.

Snow flies in the air as he sidesteps into a snow-crusted sapling to keep upright. "What was that for? I was being nice to you."

I laugh. "I was too. I really meant to knock you over. You're just too..." I huff and give him another push. "...heavy."

He doesn't sidestep this time. His laugh is full and deep and loud in the woods, and I want to swoon. He takes my hand and pulls me behind him through the silent, snowy forest. And I let him.

An hour later, we've visited about half the farms in town. At

Erkki's father's place, torches send golden flickers of light across the snow, illuminating it against the dark blue night above.

Another group of ale-tasters tumble out of the open door just as our party moves up. Several of the guys stagger more than walk, and one red-cheeked girl completely dissolves with giggles as soon as she's off the steps. Another girl pulls her towards a waiting sleigh.

One more trio steps out of the main house, and the man in the middle grins as he talks to the men flanking him. Until they see me and nudge him.

I halt my steps, and curse the timing of our arrival. Ask's gaze moves from my face to Cian's arm around my waist, and his lopsided grin drops.

Cian pulls me even closer as Ask nods in our direction. I return his greeting, but his stony mask hurts more than I'm willing to admit. I swallow down the emotion threatening to choke me.

What's done is done. I married Cian to save Finn, and I won't regret that.

Not even for Ask's sake.

Ingerid and Liisa have already disappeared inside, and I hurry to follow. But when I get to the stone steps where Erkki's sister greets the rest of our group, Cian pulls me aside.

I slip on the trampled snow by the door, and grip his arms to stay upright. He slides both arms around my waist, and my breath catches in my lungs. "What are you doing?"

Ingerid's laughter comes from inside the house, followed by cheers and whistles. Cian chuckles and pulls me much closer than necessary. "I thought we should take advantage of the fact that you're still on your feet."

I roll my eyes, but a laugh slips out despite my effort, steaming into the cold air like frosty smoke. "I am very steady on my feet, thank you very much!"

In the soft torchlight, his wolfish grin makes my stomach tumble. "I can fix that."

I'm about to ask how, but he's already leaned down to cut off my words with a kiss—and the only thing steady is my desperate grip on his shoulders as the world falls away.

CHAPTER 22

I stumble down the stairs after only a few hours of sleep. Darkness lurks beyond the frosted window panes, and a chill seeps through the walls. But downstairs, a lamp flickers cheerily in the middle of the table, next to three untouched porridge bowls. Liisa's face is buried in her folded arms on the table, and even Ingerid's smile is dimmer than usual when she hands me a stoneware mug.

I don't know if I can drink more wine after last night. I wrinkle my nose at the thought, then wince as the movement aggravates my already pounding temples.

Ingerid shakes her head. "It shouldn't make you feel worse. It's watered down."

I wrap my hand around the warm mug and thank her, and my first sip is not so bad. I nod at Liisa's bushy head as she's neither moved nor spoken. "How much did she drink last night?"

Ingerid grimaces. "She didn't keep her sips small enough."

Liisa groans loudly but doesn't lift her head. "I did! At first."

Ingerid's chuckle is a faint echo of her laugh. "I'm sure

whoever challenged you to that competition feels just as bad this morning."

Liisa huffs, voice muffled. "Worse. He was drunk when we started."

The warm wine *does* help my headache. At least a little. "I don't remember a competition?" I look to Ingerid for an explanation.

She pulls out the bench and sits, but some of the sparkle returns to her eyes. "Yeah, you were a little preoccupied, I heard. This was after we ran into Ask and Cian made a show of pulling you off to the side of the building for... well, not socializing." Her eyes say everything her words don't, and I choke on my wine.

"He did not! I mean, that's not why he did that." My cheeks burn from Ingerid's smirk, and then worse as memories of Cian's mouth on mine pushes through my foggy brain. His hands clasped around my waist, his strong fingers removing my scarf so he could drop more kisses down my neck. His—

Ingerid laughs into her own wine mug. "Uh, yeah, you didn't see the look he sent Ask. I'm pretty sure that's *exactly* why he did it."

"That was *before* I did my competition, and Ingerid's right." Liisa finally lifts her head from her table, looking about as green as I feel. She rolls her eyes in my direction, then immediately recoils, and presses a hand to her forehead. "What's actually going on with you and Cian?"

I down a giant gulp of mulled wine, but I can't cherish the warmth sliding down my throat. Because once this cup is empty, I'll have no excuse not to face my sisters' raised eyebrows.

Beyond the frosted window panes, the world is still dark, and I still need to explain what I can't possibly do adequately. That my childhood was a series of wild stories to hide cuts and bruises from our neighbors. That marrying Cian is only a means to end that for Finn. Or, at least a means to give him the company of a friend at night.

Why is this so hard? "We're... married."

"What?" Ingerid's screech makes Liisa cover her ears and whimper. Wine slops out of the mug as Ingerid slams it onto the table. "You married him? When did that happen? How? There haven't been any banns read?"

I really need less watered down wine for this conversation, because what do I tell her? I can't let them know he's a faerie.

Liisa scowls now, actually scowls. But it's not the anger in her eyes that slays me, it's the hurt. I recall my very real terror the night I found her dancing with Cian, how I told her he was dangerous, involved with someone else. The same man I've just confessed to be my husband. "Liisa, I really did think he wasn't safe that night. I thought he would hurt you, us. But then... he didn't, and..." I sigh and tell the truth. "I... really liked him."

Liisa huffs. "Yeah, I noticed that." It's the weakest explanation in the world, nowhere near enough, and we both know it.

"But what about you and Ask?" Ingerid's brow furrows. "I thought you wanted him to pursue you?"

I did. Oh, how I did! But only until I saw that wicked bruise on Finn's cheekbone and realized I could ease his pain. I don't have an answer for Ingerid that won't require an enormous suspense of disbelief. "I really like Cian, and... he made me an offer I couldn't resist." *And I made a bargain with a faerie.*

Liisa snorts and pushes her porridge bowl further away, a disgusted look on her face. "What was that? A dance?" She has every right to be angry with me, and even if Cian wasn't dangerous, telling them what he really is will lead nowhere good. What if they think I've lost my mind?

Ingerid hasn't touched her porridge since my revelation, instead her gray eyes are focused on me. "That doesn't quite seem like enough for you to marry him. And why wouldn't you tell us? Without the banns, are those even legal vows? Did he just…"

She doesn't need to finish that sentence, it's not uncommon for men to promise marriage to a woman just to get her dowry, or where there's no dowry, simply a bedmate. My stomach rumbles, but the lump in my throat makes it impossible to think of food. "I was worried about what you'd think of me."

I still am. And as for the legality? I didn't think of that, but I'm thinking of it now.

"You know we'd love you regardless." Ingerid's smile is a bit stiff, but her gaze is sincere. Would it be the same if she knew the truth?

I SHIFT into a cat in the evening and stay with Finn until morning. Then I trek across the snow in the dark to the hollow where Cian waits, followed by our attempts to make it through the cabin and up the stairs to my room without waking anyone. And without pausing too long to kiss.

We fail quite a bit at that.

I don't get violently ill again, I realize that as long as I visit Finn right before he goes to sleep and leave just as he begins to stir, I get only a headache.

An ailment Cian is more than happy to help me remedy—by planting kisses along my jaw as we sink back onto the bed. Or massage my temples with his strong fingers. Or kissing every inch of my face and neck until all traces of the headache are gone.

Flushed from the memory of this morning's remedy, I finish dinner early and take the stairs to my room in three steps.

Cian is sprawled on my bed with a smirk playing on his lips.

This room has no crackling fire, but the warmth in his gaze makes me want to fan my face all the same.

Surely the way he pulls me in without so much as a word is magic? I sink onto the bed and he tugs me down next to him. I let out a contented sigh as his fingers work their way through my braids until he can run them through my curls. His lips press to my temple.

"Cian?"

"Mhm?" His murmur against the side of my head makes goosebumps spring out across my neck.

"How did you meet Finn?" The words escape on the breath that whoosh out of my lungs as a kiss meets my collarbone.

He drops another on my throat. "It's not the happiest of stories, Saoirse."

I press my lips to his dark blonde head. "I didn't think it would be."

Cian sighs. "My father died when I was young, and my mother married again, a human from the Northwoods. Their bliss was short-lived when he was badly injured in a logging accident a few years later. When he didn't make it, my mother…" He pulls in a deep breath, and I can guess his next words by the tension in his shoulders. "My mother died from grief."

What must it be like to love someone enough that your heart gives out at the loss of them? My heart aches for his mother, and I swallow down the urge to cry. "And Finn?"

His chest rises and falls with a heavy breath. "I didn't know she left a child behind until this year." His eyes close, and I run my fingers through his hair.

Green eyes meet mine again. "When I found him, I thought I would just bring him back to Faerie with me. But Finn isn't magical, so I can't bring him. And because I'm the ruler of Faerie, I cannot be gone long enough to give him a home here. I've tried, Saoirse. Keeping him company at night has been the best I could do." He swallows. "Until now."

He pulls me closer, and we lie there for a long time just holding each other. Much later, he gives me a quick kiss before I shift into a cat. He says no more about his efforts to save Finn, and no tears slip from his glassy eyes, but I feel the ache in his soul. The same ache that echoes in mine later, as I spot the angry scrape across Finn's neck as he shifts in sleep.

There has to be another way for him to live.

There has to be more I can do.

CHAPTER 23

Throughout the darkened Northwoods, church bells sound the arrival of Yuletide.

Inside our cheery cabin Liisa munches on a gingersnap cookie while Ingerid pours mulled wine into cups. The heavenly aroma of smoked, salted lamb, mashed swedes, and tart lingonberry jam fills the room.

I've kept an eye on the cabin next to ours. As soon Master Johannes is deep enough in his cups, I'll go over to get Finn. Yuletide might be a day his uncle chooses to forget, but it doesn't need to be for Finn.

Another hour does it, and I sneak across the alley to knock on his door. Three knocks later Finn cracks it open, his lips tilting at the corners. "Miss Saoirse? What are you doing here?"

"I'm here to ask you to come celebrate with us." I return his smile, pushing down the grief that my offer is so temporary.

Hope glints in his eyes for a moment, but then it dims. "Master Johannes won't be pleased with that." As if speaking of the devil brings him forth, the man shouts from inside the cabin.

I steady my heart and make a quick decision. "Wait here." I

slip past Finn, into a cabin that smells worse than usual. In the main room Finn's uncle and tormentor is slouched on a bench. As I walk in, he tips up the stoneware jug pressed to his lips. tilting his head back, his Adam's apple bobs as he gulps the drink down. He tosses the jug in the direction of the table and misse. By some miracle the stoneware doesn't break.

Clearly it's not his first drink tonight—his shirt is already untucked from his breeches, and his eyes are a bit glassy. He's younger and handsomer than he deserves to be, and his lips tip up in a smirk when he sees me.

I lower in a curtsy, my hands fisting my skirts to keep them from touching the filthy dirt floor. "I'd like to take Finn off your hands tonight, if you don't mind." I lick my lips and hate the lies that spill from them. "You have such a big task caring for a child all year, surely you deserve a night off?"

He grunts, grabs another jug from the table and takes a swig from it. "Ah, yes, that I do. He's a lot more trouble than he's worth."

I ignore his selfish lies and plaster a smile on my face. "Thank you, Master Johannes. I'll have him back to you tomorrow."

I feel his eyes on my back as I leave and ignore the shiver down my spine. Then I'm at Finn's side, slipping my hand into his as I pull him across the alley. Cian waits for uson the stone steps, coatless and seemingly unbothered by the cold. His eyes are heated as they meet mine, but the look softens to pure contentment as they land on Finn.

He crouches down. "I'm Cian, Miss Saoirse's..." he hesitates, "...friend. I'd like you and I to be friends, too."

Finn tucks himself closer to me, but he nods.

Cian straightens, leans forward and presses a kiss to my cheek. The chaste touch shouldn't catch the breath in my lungs. But it does, and the shiver down my spine this time is of a completely different nature.

Ingerid fills the wooden wash tub with warmed water and not long after, Finn is clean and dressed in an outfit Liisa made him. He looks like a different child as he exclaims over the fragrant juniper twigs in the corners of the room and the dried apple-slice garlands. Tears press behind my eyes, and Cian's fingers curl around mine as we watch Finn bite into a warm gingersnap cookie shaped like a pig.

Ingerid hustles him over to the table where our mouth-watering dinner awaits. Tallow candles burn in every window, and the cheer and love around our table is real, and true. And magic.

And maybe magic won't always be the worst of my memories?

CHAPTER 24

As morning slips over the still-dark Northwoods, I trip downstairs to check on Finn.

Curled up on the bench by the hearth, his face is relaxed in sleep. The blanket slips down from his shoulder as he stirs, and I tiptoe close enough to tug it back up.

No breath has given life to the embers in the hearth, and there's a chill in the room.

Finn mumbles in his sleep, and my heart aches. I lean down and touch my lips to his hair. And for one short moment, I let myself dream of a world where this could be our life. Me waking early to find him snuggled in peace, safe from harm.

The door creaking open tears me out of a dream better forgotten. Finn won't be mine, now or ever. I need to be content with keeping him company as a cat.

I look up to find Ingerid, red-cheeked and smiling, as she puts town a bucket of fresh goat's milk, and shuts the door behind her. Her eyes twinkle as she greets me. "Merry Yuletide, Saoirse."

I return her greeting and toss another glance over my shoulder to the sleeping child. How I wish this peaceful slumber could be his always. "I should go back upstairs, unless you need help down here?"

Ingerid unwraps her shawl from around her neck and smirks at me. "Leave your poor husband alone up there, did you?" My cheeks burn, but it's not like she doesn't know where he sleeps. She shakes her head. "I'm not in desperate need of help, you can go back upstairs."

"You'll keep an eye on Finn?"

She dips her head, and her eyes sparkle. "I'll even feed him when he wakes, in case you get…occupied."

I slink back upstairs with my cheeks and ears on fire. Entering my room, Cian's smirk makes it no better. I feel his gaze on me as I shut the bedroom door, and it doesn't take much to convince me to crawl back in under the covers with him.

Nor to forget all about Finn's breakfast.

WHEN I COME DOWNSTAIRS, the table is decked with the best foods we can afford—pickled fish, head cheese, fresh bread, and sweet butter. Finn's tired eyes light up when he sees the spread, and I make sure he gets to eat as much as he wants. His reaction makes it clear Master Johannes's house has no tradition for such a spread, Yuletide or none.

As I refill Finn's cup for the third time, he shakes his head and pats his stomach. His cheeks are rosy and his eyes shine, and I wish this was his life always.

AFTER BREAKFAST, I run an errand for Ingerid. Cian has returned to faerie, and Liisa and Finn are laughing themselves silly over some little game only they know.

The sun rises as I strap on my skis, and the colorful sky tints the snow with soft yellows and oranges. I push off down the hill to town, the air fresh and icy cold against my cheeks. My heart feels light and buoyant.

Until I recognize the hulking figure waiting for me at the bottom of the hill. "Ask?"

He turns, but his lopsided grin is nowhere to be found. I want to squirm as he regards me with serious brown eyes. "You're alone today?"

I nod, a knot in my stomach as I recall Cian pulling me off to the side for a kiss meant only to make this kind man jealous. From his cool demeanor, I'm guessing it worked. He looks away, and I follow his gaze to a group of women whose voices have suddenly gone quiet. They all stare at us.

Or at me?

One woman with a shawl wrapped tightly under her sturdy chin whispers to the one beside her. But her voice carries on the wind, and I catch the tail end of her words.

"... Master Johannes's boy."

I frown. Does she mean Finn? I turn to Ask's drawn face. "Are they talking about Master Johannes?"

His eyes widen. "You don't know? I thought... I thought that was why you were here."

My breakfast curdles in my stomach. "What is it I don't know?"

"One of his drinking buddies found Master Johannes this morning."

"Found?" He wasn't missing. He'd been in his cabin just last night, perfectly healthy aside from a few too many drinks. I press my pole into the snowy ground, needing to lean on it for support.

Ask's lips thin, and he shifts uncomfortably. "He's dead, Saoirse."

No.

Shock clamps my fingers tighter around the pole. Was I the last to see him alive? But I don't dare tell Ask that. Not with this many eager ears around. I don't want anyone to talk. Not when the child he looked after is with me. "Where?"

Ask nods to the side of the hill I've just slid down, to a hollow where a group of men are gathered. My lungs constrict. "Outside? Why was he outside on Yuletide?"

Ask shrugs. "They say he was meeting some men at the tavern, but he never showed up."

"And they never looked for him?" Is that shrill voice mine?

"Saoirse?" Ask's face swims in and out of focus. Darkness crouches in on me, blurring the edges of my vision. The pole pushes into my stomach, and then strong arms wrap around me. Ask's voice is in my ear, but I can't decipher his words, can't focus on them apart from the increased chatter from the group of women.

If Finn's uncle is dead, what will happen to him? Will he be sent to another relative who will treat him as badly? Will I have given up the future I need only for a few days of relief for him?

"What about the little boy?" I croak the words into Ask's chest.

"He has kin farther south. I imagine they'll send him down there as soon as the Yuleday celebrations are over."

A fist clutches my heart. *They're taking him away.*

Of course they are. He'll have to live the way I did, until he's old enough to run away. And there's nothing I can do about it. There's not an official in this town who will let him live with an unmarried woman of no relation.

I'm suddenly aware of Ask's rubbing my shaking shoulders as I sob in his arms. I need to calm down. I pull in a shuddering breath, but it takes three more to stop crying. I reluctantly pull back, noticing damp spots on Ask's coat, and hoping they're only tears. "I'm so sorry."

He shakes his head. "Don't think about it."

But the thought I can't push away is that a child I've come to love will leave me so soon. And that when he does, I'm unlikely to see him again.

My heart cracks open, and another sob pushes its way over my lips.

"Are you that close to the boy?" Ask pulls off his mittens, shoving them inside his coat. His solid, workworn hand reaches towards me, but his fingers are gentle as he wipes the tears from my cheeks. He hesitates. "You could take him in? I'm sure this kin has no interest in the boy." He must see my confusion, because he keeps talking. "When his parents died, Master Johannes was the only one who showed any interest. But that time there was some land involved. This time there's no property."

I shake my head. "I can't..." My voice breaks. "I can't take him in on my own, they wouldn't let me and Liisa."

He swallows, shifting again. "But me and you? They'd let us take him in, if we were married?"

My stomach drops, and I close my eyes against the onslaught of regret.

I want to say yes. Ask is the future I wanted. And if I married him, surely, they'd let Finn stay. But I'm no longer free to marry anyone. I shake my head. "I need to get back to Finn, to tell him."

Ask's eyes widen. "He's at your cabin?"

I nod. Finn is at my cabin, playing with Liisa. And marrying his brother might have made it possible for me to keep him company at night before, but now?

Cold washes over my skin as I realize what I've really given up—I'll have to watch Finn move away, knowing I can no longer take him in.

And what will Cian do? Will he go with Finn?

I take another step back from Ask, swiping at my runny nose with my mitten. "I need to get back."

Ingerid's errand isn't that pressing. Not anymore. Not when Finn will leave.

CHAPTER 25

I shove my skis and pole into the snowbank by the wall and move towards the stone slab in front of the door. Then I stop.

How can I go in there and tell Finn that his uncle has died? As much as the man terrorized him, he's still his uncle. Surely he'll grieve him? And before that shock can even settle, there's the other message I need to give him.

The one that sits like a rock under my breastbone, making it difficult to breathe. Finn will have to leave—to live with strangers who didn't want him when he was an infant, and who surely won't want him now. And I've messed up my one chance to save him.

I pull in a deep breath and step towards the house.

"Saoirse, why are you crying?" Cian walks out from the alley and steps between me and the door, between me and a conversation I don't want to have.

I pull off my mittens and wipe the away the moisture I didn't realize coated my cheeks.

"What happened?" His face pales as he looks towards the cabin. "Is Finn… Did anything happen to him?"

I shake my head. "Not yet."

The curse he growls out isn't one I'm familiar with. "What the hell does that mean?"

I try to answer, but the emotion clogging my throat won't let me. "Finn, he…" I sob. "His uncle… died."

Cian stills. "He was no friend of yours, was he?"

I shake my head, wiping my mitten across my cheeks, trying to still the tears. "No, but Finn will leave to live with his kin farther south."

Cian's green eyes hold mine for an eternity before he closes them. When he looks at me again, something is shuttered in his eyes. I want to ask him when he reaches for me. But instead of the embrace I so desperately need, he only takes my arm and leads me up the steps. "Come, wife. Let's go tell him."

INGERID MEETS us at the door. Her gaze moves between us and she frowns. "Saoirse, what happened?" I shake my head and move past her, into the room. I can't say these words more than twice. Cian pauses to talk to her, but his words are low, and the only thing I make out is Ingerid's gasp.

I watch the smile blooming on Finn's face as Liisa speaks to him, and I hate what I'm about to do. Cian's hand grasps my waist. "I'll do it."

I shake my head. "He doesn't know you." His sharp intake of breath makes me amend my words. "Not as a man, Cian."

He grunts, and I step over to the place where two people I love sit on the goat pelts by the fire. I lower to the floor next to them. "Finn. I need to tell you something."

"What, Miss Saoirse?" The light in his green eyes dim a little as he takes in my sober expression. He looks up at Cian and shrinks back a little. I turn to see my husband leaned against the wall opposite, arms crossed and brows lowered in a thunderous scowl. I'd shrink back, too.

I turn my attention back to the boy watching me with uncertain eyes.

"Finn, something happened to Master Johannes."

He scrunches up his face. "What?"

"He died last night."

A series of reactions pass over Finn's face, then it crumples and he throws himself into my arms. I don't know what I expected, but it's not this. And I certainly didn't expect the warmth spreading in my chest.

Or the crushing ache that follows it.

I rest my cheek against Finn's hair and meet Cian's pained gaze—and I'm certain he feels the ache, too.

Hours after Finn has cried himself to sleep on the bench, I lie awake. I stare into the darkness of the room, trying not to let it join forces with the one inside me.

I think Cian is asleep, too, until he turns towards me and crushes me against his chest. His kisses are wild and hot, and like nothing I've ever felt from him before. When they finally slow, every inch of my skin is on fire under his hands.

And then, his murmur against my throat turns the blood in my veins to ice. "I need to return to my kingdom."

I push against his chest, stop his slow exploration of my collar bone, and scramble out from under him. "What do you mean you need to return?"

His eyes are hazy, and for a moment the air is filled only with our heavy breaths. I want so badly to forget about his words, to pull him back down to me. But I swallow that desire, hold my ground, and repeat my question.

He clears his throat and the hazy look in his eyes fades. "There's a situation that requires my attention, and I can't promise I'll be back here anytime soon."

"So you're leaving me?" My voice is small, like a child's. But his words sting worse than frost-nipped skin thawing.

He sits up, eyes wide with alarm. His hair mussed from my fingers and skin still flushed. If our conversation had been about anything else, I don't think I could have stopped myself from diving back into his embrace. But my heart aches, and my eyes fill with tears.

He curses. "Saoirse. I wanted to bring you with me."

For a moment, my heart feels lighter, the air warms, and the sting of frost is soothed. Then I remember what he's really proposing. "You wanted me to go with you to Faerie?" How could he think I could go with him to Faerie when Finn is here?

My grandmother's voice sounds in my ear. *Don't trust the faeries. Don't go where they ask. Don't exchange a vow with one.*

It's a little too late for that, grandmother.

I run a hand over my disintegrated braid—undone by Cian's fingers while his mouth undid me. He watches my face as if he can read my thoughts. "You wouldn't have come with me."

I sit all the way up, cheeks hot as I straighten my nightshirt and rake shaky fingers through my hair. "Of course, I wouldn't have. What made you think I could come with you? I can't just traipse off to Faerie. I have responsibilities here."

A frown mars his beautiful brow, and I want to reach out and kiss it smooth. But the haziness is completely gone from his gaze now. "Why would you not go with your husband?" His voice is so cool, so distant.

Desperately, I search his face for a trace of the man whose heated gaze just minutes ago made my skin feel like it could melt right off my body. The man who made me lose myself in his kisses. But all I see staring back at me are the dark green eyes of a faerie I've just crossed.

Don't trust the faeries.

I swallow. "I am not your property."

He flinches. "I never said you were." A curse flies from his mouth—harder, sharper than the one before. He rubs a hand down his face, as if I'm the one being difficult.

But I know what's coming. I've been here before, and my heart already shrivels in my chest. Why does no one stay for me? Why am I never enough?

Perhaps my grandmother didn't leave of her own volition, but I was deserted all the same. And my aunt chose her demons over me when I needed her most—punished me for the strain of a life she chose and I didn't.

I push down the sob wringing its way out of me. "Then why do you act like I'm yours to command?"

"I DON'T!" He roars the words, and I flinch.

This discussion is over. Maybe more than just this discussion. *Maybe us.*

His hand slashes through the air, and my shoulders hunch to brace for an impact that doesn't come.

"So, that's it? You'd stay here rather than come with me to a world where I am the prince? You still refuse to believe I won't trick you?" He moves off the bed. At his full height he looks every bit the Faerie royal he is.

I swallow down the persistent sob, run a hand down my face, and wish we could have this conversation on more sleep. "Why don't you understand that you being the prince in another world doesn't matter to me? I need to stay here with Finn."

But will I even be given the chance to stay with Finn now?

"We can't take him with us, can we?"

His Adam's apple bobs. "No." Everything about him stiffens with the word—his stance, the set of his shoulders, his gaze.

I sniffle, hating the vulnerability it betrays. "And who did you think would stay with him? Were you going to marry Liisa, too, so she could look after him in my place?"

He blanches. "How can you say that?"

I shrug. "That was your solution last time, wasn't it, to marry me when you could no longer show yourself at Finn's?"

He shakes his head, and his shoulders expand as he draws in a deep breath. "That's not…" But his lips clamp over the words I need.

He shakes his head, his gaze on the rumpled sheets beside me. "We'd have asked them to keep an eye on him so you could come with me."

I stand up and pull the blanket from the bed in a weak attempt at modesty. As if the woven fabric can somehow cover the vulnerability in my hasty movements.

I'm not ready for the words I'm about to say. I don't want to say them at all, but I don't have a choice, do I? "I've done a lot of things you've asked. I slept in a bed with you, I married you, I learned to shift for you, but I will never leave my world for you."

I mean my town, the Northwoods, the human world. But as the words freeze on the air and clatter to the floor between us, they sound like they mean more than that.

Cian clenches his jaw, and irritation eclipses the hurt in his eyes.

I take a step back from him. "You better not try to force me. I don't care if faerie marriages allow husbands to gallivant their wives around at will."

He laughs, a bitter laugh, and goosebumps break out on my arms. He shakes his head as the corner of his lips turn up. "*We* have no such rules, no. But this is a human marriage."

I don't understand the distinction, but does it matter? I study the man before me as tears well in my eyes. No. Not the man. *The faerie.* "When do you leave?"

"Tonight."

I gasp. Is he serious? "You thought I'd agree to skip off to Faerie tonight? With no notice?"

He doesn't answer, just stands there, so immovable, and so...
inhuman.

I pull in a breath through lungs that ache as though I've
sprinted through the woods in midwinter. A band tightens
around my chest. "Don't you understand that I have a life here?
A..." my voice breaks a little, "child that needs me?"

His jaw clenches. "And don't *you* understand that I have a
kingdom to rule?"

"Since when is that more important than Finn?" Than
staying here with me?

Why, if he's gone to all this trouble to protect Finn, is he so
ready to leave him on his own now?

Cian's curse is bitter on the air. "Saoirse. If I leave, you can..."
He grits his teeth, then looks sick. "You can marry the blacksmith's son, and my brother can live with you."

My heart breaks at the look in his eyes. I want to plead with
him, to ask him to choose me, like I've chosen him so many
times.

I need to.

But I can't. Not when he looks at me without warmth in his
gaze. As if we're strangers. *Are we?* The thought snarls around
my heart, cuts off its blood flow, and shrivels it up to nothing.

This is why I didn't want him. Why I should have chosen
Ask all along. Like I would have, had Cian not waltzed into my
life with his magical charm and disarming protectiveness of his
brother.

His brother whose fate I've lived. How could I not choose
Cian when it gave me the chance to make a difference for Finn?
"You already married me. That doesn't change just because you
leave."

"Human marriages aren't valid in Faerie." His words clamp
around my chest like a vise, and my head spins. Is that true? Did
he marry me without telling me our marriage was invalid where
he has been returning nightly?

But I want to slap myself even as the thought appears. Have I learned nothing from these past few weeks?

I spent a decade thinking my grandmother's stories were just that—folklore passed from mother to daughter for generations. And I was wrong, because Cian, his light, his kisses, his solid presence, was real.

The way I fell helplessly in love with him when I knew so much better, was real. The way he's breaking my heart into bloodied shards right now is so, so real.

I want to scream, but as I open my mouth no sound escapes.

I should never have let him curl himself around my heart, tempting it to beat for more than just the escape from wounds that will not heal. And yet, had I ever a chance against his sardonic smirks, his small acts of kindness, or the infuriating attraction that sprang up between us? Against magic?

The magic that now makes it impossible to pull in a full breath.

The magic that aches like hellfire through my body.

Magic isn't what I need, has *never* been what I needed.

I need...

I swallow and try to shut him out, to close the heart I'd begun to open for him. No, not begun. The doors are wide open, too open to do anything but leave my heart bleeding as his silence plunges its arrows into it.

Don't trust the faeries.

I was a fool not to heed the warnings in the stories.

"I'm sorry you can't accompany me. I wish you luck." His words are smooth, his voice as melodious as ever, but all his beautiful speech brings is hurt. Another arrow. Another wound.

And then, he's gone.

I buckle to my knees. I don't know what hurts more—the way he yelled at me or his careless dismissal. I can't even cry. Dry sobs heave my chest as I try to gain my composure.

I give up when voices float up through the floorboards.

Once I'm dressed, I join them for breakfast.

I brush off Ingerid's comment about my red eyes. I flinch when she asks if Cian will join us, and understanding settles on her face. "I thought I heard you fighting." Her voice is soft as she reaches for me, but I shrink away from her hug.

If I feel her arms around me, I will lose it completely, and I can't do that. Finn deserves happy memories today. As happy memories as he *can* have before I have to tell him.

AFTER BREAKFAST, we slide down the hill to town. Ingerid and I remain on the sidelines after our first trip down, but Liisa and Finn go again and again.

No horse-drawn sleighs will move about today, and with last night's snowfall, every child in town has trudged up the hill to slide back down on whatever improvised sled they have available. The air fills with their whoops of laughter as they descend down the hill, and more often than not, tumble into a pile at the bottom. Softly falling snow sparkles in the glow of the torches, turning the scene magical.

But the Yuletide cheer around me does nothing but exaggerate my heartache. Nothing but highlight the fact that Cian didn't even wait to leave. As the sun sets in the afternoon, I give up. If his plan had been to say goodbye, he would have by now. The chaos outside has calmed down, and he still hasn't appeared.

The Northwoods is covered in the velvety winter darkness, but inside the tar-blackened walls, a fire crackles in the hearth. Ingerid puts together an easy supper for the four of us. I don't know what is decided about Finn, so I tell him nothing.

But when Liisa brings Finn outside for one more turn down the hill, Ingerid can no longer hold back her curiosity. "Saoirse.

I know you don't want to talk about it, but I'm worried about you. Why did Cian leave?"

Her eyes are the kind that easily pulls my secrets, but tonight I have none to tell. The truth hurts too much to speak out loud.

Cian is gone to Faerie without me, leaving me only with the knowledge that our marriage isn't valid there. I pick apart the cake on my plate, the buttery flavor like ashes when I put a piece into my mouth. The backs of my eyes burn, and I stand up so quickly the bench nearly tips behind me. Then I flee both the cabin and Ingerid's comfort.

Outside, I sink down on the front step. I don't care that my shirtsleeves are much too thin to keep me warm in the freezing temperatures. I don't care that the tear that steals out from my closed lids will freeze to my cheek.

Cian finally left me alone, so I could marry Ask. Just like I wanted when we met.

Except, this isn't what I ever wanted.

I wanted a husband who would stay by my side and keep me safe. Who'd build a stable home for me and our children. Falling for a faerie who'd ruin my chance to marry well and then leave me behind on a whim wasn't in those plans.

Don't trust the faeries. Don't follow them anywhere, or let them secure a promise from you. My grandmother's voice fills the cracks in my heart the way it used to fill the dark winter mornings. The crinkles at the corners of her eyes deepen as her warm voice banishes the chill deep inside me.

I close my eyes and feel her familiar tug on the curl that used to slip free from my braids. The one that still escapes all my attempts to tame it, years beyond the last time she was here to pin it back in.

But when I open my eyes, the tug is only in my memories. And I'm still cold.

Still alone.

CHAPTER 26

Finn's smile lights up his face and warms my sore heart. He's already snuggled up on the bench, when I pad gracefully down the stairs as his cat. The light from the still burning lamp illuminates his face like relief lighting his voice. "You came back!"

He moves to get out from the warm blanket cocoon, but I'm faster as I sprint across the floor and jump up on the bench. The innate grace of my cat body, now that I finally have the hang of it, never fails to amaze me.

Once I'm curled up next to him, Finn laughs quietly and tucks me close to his side. His little hand runs through the fur on my back.

"I'm so glad you're here. I didn't want to go to sleep alone." He whispers into my fur, breath warm and voice so vulnerable I want to cry. It makes the shattering ache in my chest worth it. Finn needs me, and I won't let him down now.

"Miss Saoirse told me Master Johannes died, so I have to stay here now. I don't know how long." Finn prattles on, blessedly unaware of my heart breaking beside him.

I'm suddenly thankful for a body that can't speak. Finn

doesn't expect me to say anything, and my cat face doesn't give away emotions as easily as my human face. I don't even know what I would tell him if I could.

It's been less than a day since his uncle died. Will they send a letter, or just send Finn away without a certain answer from his kin?

Finn blows out the lamp and slides further down under the covers. His one hand cradles my back. "I sleep so much better when you're here."

Soon his breathing evens out. But I can't sleep.

The darkness of a future I don't know swirls in my mind. I have no way of knowing what will happen to Finn, but I know what has already happened to me.

Cian tricked me just like my grandmother warned. Married me here and left for a kingdom where he wasn't tied to me. With a sickening crumpling in my gut, I remember the faerie girl I saw in the hollow. I can't compete with beauty like that. Does she visit him in faerie too? Or worse, what if they're married there?

My heart aches while my stomach keeps churning.

Never trust a faerie.

What a fool I've been.

CHAPTER 27

Without Cian's headache remedies tempting me to dawdle in bed, it's earlier than usual when I walk through the village under the dancing colors in the dark sky.

The morning is crisp and clear, and as the colors cease, the velvety dark above comforts in its very darkness. Snow crunches under my boots, and cold seeps in through woolen scarves and mittens.

Up ahead of me, a figure pulls a loaded sled behind him as he moves slowly through the snow towards me. I know him instantly, even before I hear the timbre of his voice as he stops to talk to an old woman hunched over her front gate.

Ask bumbles towards me like the giant he is, his shoulders wider than the other boys', his presence steadier, his temper cooler. All things that drew me to him. Under his thick coat, I imagine his muscled forearms are still streaked with soot from yesterday's work at the smithy.

He doesn't have Cian's lithe build, nor would he be considered ethereally beautiful on his best day, but he's definitely handsome.

With our history, I should melt under his gaze, long for his touch.

I don't now. But maybe that can change?

His brown eyes are warm as they meet mine, and torchlight glints off copper strands in his dark hair. Maybe it isn't too late for us? Maybe I can still have the safe future I've longed for since the day my grandmother died.

You're married, Saoirse.

But I push the thought away. *Is it really a marriage if only one party is bound by its vows?*

I should ask Cian that. Except that I can't, because he's off gallivanting without me in Faerie. Pain twists another blade in my gut.

The man I should have chosen tilts his head as he looks down at me. His gaze doesn't make my insides flop like Cian's does, and perhaps his touch has never quite felt as magical as the faerie's. *But I don't need magic. I need safety.*

And I know if Ask marries me, he'll do whatever he can to keep me safe.

"How are you holding up, Saoirse?" His voice is dark, almost husky, and it should make my senses tingle. I wait a moment to give my body time to catch up.

When it doesn't, I answer him before he thinks I didn't hear him. "Still waiting to hear what's going to happen with Mater Johannes's boy. Do you know anything?"

He shakes his head. "I haven't heard anything. I'll tell you if I do." I nod. Though who knows when anyone will get around to writing that letter? "That man who carried you off after you had too much to drink at the tavern, he's the same one I saw you with last week, isn't he? What's his name?"

I swallow down the bile rising in my throat. I don't want to talk about the faerie who tricked me into marrying him. "Cian." His name grates across my vocal cords, pierces open the scab in my chest.

"That's what it was. Lucky man. Speaking of engagements…" He trails off as frozen air seeps into my stomach. *No. No. No. This isn't happening.* "I asked Kari Bakken to be my wife."

"What?" The word is a squeak, but I can't help it. Couldn't he have found someone a little less perfect? Someone I hadn't spent so much time comparing myself to and come up short?

"She said yes." His words are a suckerpunch, and pain radiates from my solar plexus. The air in my lungs freeze as loss rings its hollow bell. As every magical moment with Cian crumbles. As my head spins and nausea rises.

I chose the wrong man, and I lost my chance. Honey-blonde curls and laughing blue eyes dance in my mind as Kari taunts me.

"Saoirse, didn't you hear me?"

I open my eyes to Ask's concerned gaze, and tears spring to my eyes. Why am I such an idiot? "I…" My voice cracks. "I heard you. Congratulations. I have to go."

I turn and run as he calls my name behind me. But I'm full on crying now, and nothing will make me stop until I'm safely home where I can burrow my face into my pillow and never leave.

I should never have dared to believe in magic. Never let my heart fill with stupid hope, or believed the words of a deceitful faerie. If I had heeded the stories, my heart wouldn't be shattering right now. My eyes wouldn't be stinging nor my nose tingling.

But this is what magic does.

It wreaks havoc.

Why, oh why, did I trust Cian when I knew what he was?

CHAPTER 28

As soon as I step into my room, I realize I can't stay in a place filled with so many memories. I can't sleep in sheets that smell like Cian.

I close the door and move down the stairs slowly, as if death itself has settled on my shoulders. But hasn't it? The death of a marriage if nothing else. My chest aches as I enter the main room. Once I've breathed life into the glowing goals, I settle on the bench where I can stare into the flames.

I was right all along.

Safety is what I needed, always what I needed. Not magic.

And now it's too late. Ask and Kari will likely marry soon. And I will be alone, nothing but memories to keep me warm at night. Memories that can't keep me safe. Just like memories never have.

I shiver and pull my shawl tighter around my shoulders, but it's no use. There should be another jar of the mulled wine somewhere. If I can just find it.

I stand to rifle through the chest across from the hearth. After a short search and a much longer time to heat it up, my reward is in my hand.

I find my seat again just as the door bursts open. Liisa waltzes inside, tugs off a soppy shawl, and drapes it over the chest by the fire. "I saw you run up the hill, so I told her you were sick, Saoirse, but she's not very happy with you."

I cradle the mug in my hands. "Mistress Pedersen is never happy about anything."

Liisa raises her dark eyebrows. "That might be so, but she said she'll hire Kari Bakken if you don't show up tomorrow."

Just another twisting of the knife in my heart. "Kari won't need the employment, she's going to marry Ask, isn't she?" My voice quivers without my permission.

Liisa doesn't answer, and when I look up, she's tugged her lower lip between her teeth. "Where did you hear that?"

"From Ask. Did you know?" I swallow another gulp of the warm wine, hoping it will thaw the ache in my chest as much as the rest of me.

"I… I knew, but I thought you were happy with Cian. And the way he talked about you, I thought—" tears fill my eyes, and I can't hold back my sob.

Liisa dives for me, and though I desperately want to hear what he said about me, I can't stop the sobs that wrack me as I cry into her thin shoulder.

"Oh no, Saoirse. I'm so sorry, I shouldn't talk about this." Her arms wrap around me, and I think she's learned a thing or two from Ingerid over the years. Or maybe, I've just never needed her comfort like I do now.

JUST ONE MORE DAY PASSES BEFORE Ask knocks on our door to tell me what I didn't want to consider—they're sending Finn with a merchant traveling south. A merchant leaving at first light.

I kneel next to the boy I love and feel my heart break along with his. "They've found a relative you can stay with."

His face crumples as his glassy eyes turn an even deeper green. "You won't let me stay with you?"

I shake my head. "They won't let me. I'm so sorry." I wrap my arms around him and hug him until my muscles ache. All I feel is his heaving sobs and the tears soaking through my linen shirt. I don't know how my heart can take this.

It can't.

A GROUP of Travellers park their sleighs in town that night, and I walk Finn past their colorful tents and booths filled with wares. His happy chatter is almost enough to make me forget our shared heartache. "Look, Miss Saoirse, look at the horse!"

I follow Finn's wide-eyed gaze to the top of a painted chest where a wooden horse as large as a cat moves in a mechanical gallop. White linen cloth is draped under its hooves, and the shiny thread catches the torchlight until it looks just like a snowy field. It's so breathtakingly beautiful that it feels like a fist clamping around my heart.

Finn gasps. "It looks just like magic!"

The fist around my heart tightens. *Oh Cian, this is what magic does to me.*

"Don't you think it looks like magic, Miss Saoirse?" Finn's eyes are so green, so hopeful.

So like Cian's.

I nod. "See the little trees dusted with sparkles?" I crouch down next to him and point. He exclaims, and I wipe away the tear that rolls down my cold cheek into my scarf. We stay at the Traveller's booth until I think my toes will burst from the cold.

"Finn." I tug on his shoulder, and hate the way it slumps when I tell him it's time to go home. But he doesn't protest.

I tuck the juniper candies I bought from another seller into the pocket of his ill-fitted coat. That, at least, tugs a smile to his lips.

For a little while.

Too soon, we reach the tavern where I'm handing him off. I hug him tight to me and plant a kiss on his cold cheek. When I straighten, I nail the burly merchant with a glare. "Where are you taking him?"

He shrugs and mentions a town I've never heard of. "Blacksmith said to take him south in the morning with this letter to his kin." He pats his coat pocket.

I nod, even though that is nowhere near enough information. Does Ask know more?

I pull Finn in for one more hug and whisper all the words I never got to hear before I was handed off to a stranger.

How much he means to me.

How strong and kind and wonderful he is.

That I will never forget him.

He nods resolutely and turns towards his fate. A piece of my heart tears away as I watch him hunch his shoulders and trudge the last few steps to the door of the tavern.

I ache to protect him. But how? I wasn't strong enough to take him from his uncle by force, and the law cares little for what happens to orphans.

Still the need to keep him safe cracks my heart in two. I long to give him a home where he knows he is safe and loved and wanted.

That I don't have that power hurts more than Cian leaving me behind.

More than the loss of my grandmother.

It just hurts.

CHAPTER 29

Big, fluffy snowflakes twirl down from above, sparkling in the golden torchlight.

If not for the fact I should have been at the Pedersen farm long before now, I'd tip my head back to catch one on my tongue. Instead, I storm through the darkened town square, heart-sore and tired from another sleepless night.

My heart aches whenever I think of Finn, somewhere out there in the freezing Northwoods, bundled up in a sleigh with a stranger.

I couldn't sleep last night, not when he slept alone and friendless in the tavern. Not when I knew he'll likely spend the rest of his nights like I did. Until he's old enough to make it on his own, too.

I curl my bare hands into fists and tuck them under my shawl. It's nowhere near enough to shield them from the biting wind but it will have to do.

Running footsteps sound behind me, and my heart speeds up, until I hear a familiar voice call out. "Please wait up, Saoirse."

I halt my steps and turn to see Ask jog the last few feet between us, then he stops, too. He leans forward, braces his large, mittened hands on his thighs as he gasps for breath.

"I need to tell you…" He pants. "I… Kari and I aren't. We broke our engagement."

My heart stills. "What? Why?"

He looks up at me, eyes like dark syrup, so hopeful I want to drown in them. A snowflake lands on his nose, and he swipes a large mitten over it. "I think you know why."

But I can't think. My mind is a whirlwind of thoughts and questions matching the speed of the swirling snow around us. Surely he doesn't mean it's because of…

Me? I slap a hand against my chest and mouth the word.

Ask's lips turn up, and his gaze softens. "I wanted you, Saoirse. I never should have asked Kari to be my wife."

These are words I would have given anything to hear just weeks ago. Now they just make my head feel light, the air I'm breathing too thin. "I don't know what to say. When did this happen?"

Color darkens his cheekbones, and he pulls at the snowy scarf bundled around his neck.

"Did you end things *this morning?*" My stomach sinks. I don't want to be any man's consolation prize.

Ask shakes his head. "Last night."

Which makes me as good as that. But his reasons for wanting me will not change what I'm really after, will it? I will still have a strong husband to protect me, whatever the reason he's there. He'll still raise our children without the use of his fists, won't he? Even Finn?

I turn my head to follow his gaze over my shoulder, but the town square is nothing but blustering wind piling the snowdrifts high against the cabins nearby.

"I needed time to think, and I didn't want you to think you were my second choice…" His words trail off as he studies my face. I don't know what he sees there, but evidently it's not quite what he expects. "Please don't tell me I'm too late." The emotion in his voice pulls me back from my thoughts.

Is he too late?

If my marriage to Cian was never valid, I must still be free to marry Ask, right? Cian may have told the truth when he said I was a coward to choose safety over magic. But the ache that spreads in my heart just thinking of him, tells me my cowardly ways were sound.

I'd been right to value safety over magic.

I do my best to push Cian to the recesses of my mind—his magical touch and green gaze pulling me in until I was happy to drown in it, the delirious happiness I felt with him.

But unlike Cian, the man that sweeps off his mittens and gently takes my cold hands in his own large, workworn ones will not leave me to rule a foreign kingdom.

I'll be safe with Ask. I've always known this.

His thumb rubs across my hand, and though there's no simmer of magic under my skin, his touch *is* nice. Can I say yes to this?

I catch his eyes, honest, brave, and true. "This is all so sudden, Ask."

He pulls my hands to his lips, eyes still on mine. His breath warms my chilled skin. "Will you give me another chance?"

I hesitate and pull my lip between my teeth before I remember it will only chap them in this weather. His gaze drops to my mouth, and I wait for the thrill I feel when Cian sends me that same look. But it doesn't come.

"I don't want to rush anything. You were engaged to someone else just last night." *And I was married.* Which I'll need to tell him.

That lopsided smile I'm so fond of makes an appearance again. "We'll take it slow, I promise." He pulls me closer, tucking my cold hands against his chest. We're so close. If one of us leans forward... And then Ask does.

His lips press against mine in a tender kiss—and not a single spark ignites my blood. It's not a bad kiss, but it doesn't have a single magical ember.

Until it does.

Fire licks a burning path across my lips, and I pull back with a gasp.

"Saoirse, love, what's wrong?" It's Ask's voice, but not his face. I watch in horror as his skin stretches and moves and dark fur covers his lower jaw. He reaches for me, but his fingers are claws, and I shrink away.

Just like last time.

Anger digs sharp spikes into my chest, and I want to scream. Turning in a circle, I search for the faerie determined to ruin not just my first marriage, but also my second. Swirling snow makes it impossible to make out anything but shadows around us.

"What the hell is your problem?" I shout the words into the wind, but I catch Cian's mirthless chuckle on the air, and I know he can hear me.

"Saoirse, are you all right?" Ask's eyes are wide, his features returned to normal now that there's no danger of him kissing me. He follows my gaze into the storm.

"I'm fine. Can you give me a moment? I need to deal with something." *With someone.*

Fury taints my words as I yell into the darkness. "Really? You're not even going to show yourself?"

Before the last word leaves my lips, Cian is in front of me— all snapping eyes and clenched teeth. He towers over me, and his snow white shirt billows in the freezing wind. "I thought you were already married to me? Is faithfulness to your marriage vows not commonly observed in human marriages?"

Ask makes a sound behind me, but I ignore him, and stab my

finger into Cian's chest as I enunciate each word so slowly my tongue burns with the effort. "You. Left. Me."

"I had a kingdom to rule." He snarls the words as if they're a valid excuse.

Ask steps between us, disbelief jarring his voice. "You're married?"

I shake my head vehemently, pushing down the tears that threaten to clog my throat. "No, Ask, I'm not married."

Cian growls, and the curse that flies from his lips make it clear where he stands on the question. But if he was so certain we were married, maybe he shouldn't have left and all but told me to marry someone else.

I swallow the words I want to shout at him and focus my attention on Ask. "I'm not married, and I promise to think about your offer, but I.... Please give me a moment to talk to Cian."

Ask's dark eyes narrow with suspicion. It's a look so far removed from the heated one he sent me earlier, I want to cry. He does step back, though, so I grab Cian's arm and pull him several steps away. We're not really out of earshot, but I don't know how much Ask will be able to hear over the punishing wind tearing at my clothes.

"Not married, huh?" Cian's voice is icy, but he has no right to be offended.

I face him, trying to pull from the anger that surged through me seconds ago. But as my gaze settles on the man, the faerie, in front of me—all I find is grief.

"You told me human marriages aren't valid in Faerie. You left and told me to marry Ask." My voice breaks on the last word, and I hate that I can't hide my vulnerability from him.

"Saoirse." He says my name softly as if it can repair what he's broken.

I force my voice to be firm, stripping it of the emotions wreaking havoc on my heart and lungs. "Are they valid?"

His jaw clenches, and his gaze moves over my shoulder, into the raging wind. "No."

His confirmation burns like lye, and my eyes sting. How could he do this to me? And how could I be stupid enough to think I could trust a faerie? Why didn't I heed the warnings in the stories?

I swallow down the questions. "You can't expect me to keep vows I gave you when you chose to live in a place where our vows weren't valid. I'm sure you also didn't lack for company."

His face blanches. "Also? Who else did you kiss?" The hurt in his voice should make me feel good, but it doesn't. This conversation is over. *We're over.*

A single tear burns a track down my cheek, and I no longer care if he sees. I don't care about anything. "Goodbye, Cian." I turn to leave as one more tear follows the first. Then another.

"No." The word whips out with all the authority of the Faerie ruler he is.

Is he for real? I turn back to him. My face is a mess, and Cian's haughty expression blurs through the watery curtain. "What do you mean no? You can't decide that I'm not saying goodbye to you! You made your choice! It's not my fault that you don't like it!"

"I made the wrong one!" He groans, and rubs both hands down his face. "I really did want you to come with me. But with Master Johannes gone, you could marry the blacksmith and make a home for Finn. And... I thought I'd be able to forget you."

His Adam's apple bobs, and he doesn't meet my gaze. "Humans are supposed to be forgettable. Being away from you wasn't supposed to make me feel as if I'd given up air." He huffs. "I thought I could go back to see you one last time, and then I find you lip-locked with that bumbling giant of a safety charm." He gestures towards the shadow that must be Ask.

"He has a name!"

He growls. "Yes, and I'd rather I never heard it again!"

"I chose him because he doesn't make me feel like *this*!" I swipe at the tears on my face, but they can't be stopped. They flow as if I'm no longer a human girl, but an endless well of grief. "I can't feel this much, not when it has to be pain. Yes, magic feels like color and light descending on earth for the first time, but then it turns into this. And I don't want *this*. I never wanted this."

His green eyes burn into mine. "Well, *I do*. I want you."

I pull in a shaking breath and say the only words I can. "Then you're out of luck, because you can't have me."

I turn away from Cian, only to face Ask's hulking frame moving towards me through the sleet and snow. But I brush off his questions, too. I can't explain to him what he just heard and witnessed. And if Cian disappears into thin air, I won't explain that either.

I leave both men in the town square, furiously swiping at my cheeks as I march through the snow towards the scolding I'll get from Mistress Pedersen.

I don't want Cian, I meant the words I spat at him. He married me and left me behind to go rule his faerie kingdom. Even if he did it for Finn, it's not enough.

Ask's kiss might not make me feel the way a kiss ought to— even before Cian cursed him to appear a beast. His mouth against mine felt more like a warm embrace. But it doesn't matter.

I press my frozen fingers against my lips and groan into the cold night. Why is it that when the stupid faerie kisses me, I struggle to remember my own name, and when the man who'd truly be good for me does, I'd just as soon scrub the floors at the Pedersen farm?

But my craving for magic doesn't matter, it's still only brought me misery. No, Cian can't have me. I deserve a husband who can stay in my realm, where I am.

Ask will hear me out once I talk to him. He already broke off his engagement to Kari, and I'm sure he can forgive me for this morning. His kisses might improve with time once the memory of Cian's fade.

And even if they don't, I know Ask will keep me safe.

And I'll have a home for Finn.

CHAPTER 30

Ll that remains of my heart is a lump of bloody pulp, and it aches whenever I pause too long. I've polished the Pedersens's silver until every spoon looks like a mirror world of my own. I've scrubbed the floors with sand until they shine bone white— but it has changed nothing.

Cian is gone. Because I asked him to leave.

Finn is gone because I didn't save him.

I walk home through the darkness, my arms and back aching, but I find no respite from the memories. The wind brings with it a whiff of fresh pine, and Cian's words crash through the flimsily stacked barriers in my mind and floods me again with anguish.

"Well, I do. I want you."

"Then you're out of luck, because you can't have me."

And he still can't have me. Because the fact remains that I can't—can't—keep feeling like this. My grandmother's stories might not have been entirely on the mark. Cian is far kinder and much more compassionate than they ever allowed for. But he's still a faerie, bent on deceit and with no regard for how profoundly he's messed up my life.

I pass the alley, and pull my gaze away from the snow laden trees behind the cabin. I don't want to know if he's there, I don't want to remember the times when he was. I need to forget everything about him. If I can do that, then maybe, maybe my chest will no longer feel like an endless hole about to swallow me up in its vastness.

I traverse the stone steps with legs that feel like lead and push the door open. The warmth of the cabin wraps around me, and bench legs scrape as Liisa gets up from the table. I shut the door on the frigid weather outside.

"Saoirse. I was just about to eat. You'll join me, won't you?" She points to a second bowl of stew, but I shake my head. I can't even stomach the thought of food, much less the smell up close.

Her brows knit tighter over dark eyes, and the candles on the table flicker off the concern etched there. "You're so pale. Won't you please have just a little?"

With stiff fingers, I pull off layer after snowy layer of shawls and hoods. "I'm not hungry." I drape the soggy garments over the bench.

"We all miss Finn. Is that what this is?" She turns away from the food, plants both fists on her hips, and looks far too much like our oldest sister. At any other time, it would have made me laugh. But the part of me that could laugh seems eerily missing.

I shake my head as I try and fail to keep the tears at bay. They spill hot over my lashes, against my still frozen cheeks. "I can't talk about it, Liisa, please don't make me."

How can I, when just the thought of what I don't have, and can't ask for, makes my chest shatter? I never wanted to fall in love with a magical creature. I only wanted to be safe, and then, the same for Finn.

And now he's no safer than before, living among strangers, and still I've somehow torn my heart to shreds in the process.

I can't help the sob that slips out. Liisa steps forward, and her embrace says all the words I so desperately need to hear. As does the kiss she presses to my hair.

I pull away from her, sniff, and wipe another tear. We have too much to do before the wedding for me to fall apart now. "We still have sewing, don't we?"

She groans, and rubs her forehead. "Yes, so much. I don't know how we'll ever finish it."

I find the basket of work, and while Liisa finishes her supper, I embroider tiny roses into Ingerid's shirt cuffs at the other end of the table. *Erkki will probably never get the notion that he should disappear to Faerie and leave his wife behind.*

I stab my thumb with my needle and wince at the fresh pearl of blood.

If Ingerid pricked her finger while sewing her bridegroom's shirt, a blood stain would bring them happiness—so the old saying goes. I wipe the blood off on a rag.

I doubt my blood will bring her any luck, and I'm not about to damage her bridal clothes, or her chance at happiness.

Once Liisa can no longer keep her yawns at bay, she reluctantly tells me goodnight. But I don't go upstairs to my room. Instead I kneel by the hearth and watch the red glow of the coals fade.

The regret in Ask's voice haunts me as much as Cian's return. Their words swirl around in my brain, over and over until I want to scream. I'd gladly hem sheets till dawn if only my brain could have a bit of quiet.

But then I think of Finn. Recall the last night I curled up next to his still form to listen to his steady breathing. Almost without realizing it, I have shifted. My vision suddenly sharp enough to pick up the glowing embers my human eyes could no longer see.

Much later, when there's nothing left but ashes, I curl up on Finn's bunk. But as exhausted as I am, sleep will not come. And my heart aches in its absence.

Hours later, long before the sun rises, I slink down to the hollow to shift. I throw up as soon as I turn human. But unlike the last time, there is no warm hand on my neck, no strong fingers curled around my hair to keep it out of the way. No arms to hold me against a solid chest and carry me up through the alley to the cabin—only memories that ache worse than the bile that burns its way up my throat.

I walk back up to the cabin on unsteady legs, under moonlight colder than my parting words to Cian. I open the door, and my stomach quivers as I smell the porridge Ingerid stirs at the hearth. I press my lips together and will my stomach to hold onto my lunch from yesterday.

Ingerid turns from the pot to me, eyes wide. "Saoirse! What in the world were you doing outside this early? And what's that smell, are you sick?"

I nod, and unable to hold back any longer, I throw up right in front of Ingerid.

Within minutes, I'm tucked under my blankets upstairs. Ingerid is adamant I stay in bed for the day, but I have no doubt Mistress Pedersen will make good on her threat to hire Kari Bakken in my stead if I miss another day. And now she's no longer marrying Ask, she'll go gladly. Once Ingerid leaves, I get dressed again, and slip out the door.

ASK MEETS me outside the Pedersen farm again that evening, but the thrill I felt last time is replaced by a stomach filled with dread. As I sand-scrubbed the rest of the floors, I had a lot of time to think. Too much, really.

I don't ever want to see Cian again, but I also don't think I can marry Ask. Not now that I know what magic feels like. Not when I know how different the meeting of lips is when there's passion behind it. And I know what I must do.

"Saoirse." Ask reaches for my mittened hand. I fold it into his even as I know I'll have to let it go soon. That *he'll* let it go as soon as I tell him my answer. We walk into the busy street. The golden glow of torchlight illuminates the townspeople milling around us. A red-cheeked woman cradles a small child, repeatedly tugging her shawl back over the little bare fist determined to peek out into the cold. Men with strained faces that prove these dark winter days are long, and cold, and dreary—that even the cheer of Yuletide can't change that.

We've only taken a few steps when Ask pulls me away from the main-trek through town, and turns to me with a frown. "Why did Cian seem to think you were married?"

My stomach drops. The chilled wind scalds my cheeks, and the bones in my face ache. I should have known Ask would get straight to the point.

And don't I owe him that at least?

I clear my throat and pull my scarf away from my mouth. "He asked me, but then he left." It's the truth, if a partial one.

"And what about now that he's back?" Ask's face is carefully blank, so much so it must be a mask. But he was engaged to someone else days ago, surely he can't hinge all his hopes on the outcome of this conversation?

I shake my head, and bile rises in my throat as I consider my words about the man I want to forget. "He's not back. Yesterday was just…" I shrug. "I'm not getting back together with him."

Ask's shoulders lower, and his breath spills out into a cloud of white. "So you're free to be my girl? My wife?"

Sadness crushes the weak organ in my chest.

I want to say yes—I want so desperately to say yes. A month ago, I would have thrown my arms around his neck, crushed my lips to his, and… been happy to settle.

But now? "I can't."

I can't settle for the comfort of the life he could give me. Not now that I know there is more to be gained from a relationship than comfort. Not with the burning touch of Cian's lips still etched into my skin.

Not even when I know it would make my other plan so much easier.

Ask frowns as he searches my face. "What do you mean? Didn't you just say that you're not back together with Cian?"

I squirm under his scrutiny and shake my head. "I'm not."

Hurt creeps into his expression, then his jaw clenches. "You just don't want to be with me? A blacksmith's son not enough for you?"

My heart bleeds, because he's so wrong. A blacksmith's son is more than good enough for me, just not the lack of magic in his kisses. I shake my head, willing him to believe me. Needing him to. "No. You were everything I wanted."

"Were." His voice is blank, every emotion stripped away.

I nod. "I'm so sorry, Ask. I can't."

He drops my hand, and turns away without a word. I swallow down my tears as I watch him walk into the snowy wind, away from me. It's everything I deserve after stringing him along like I have. But hurting him now is kinder than hurting him every day for the rest of our lives, isn't it?

I turn away from the sight of his unyielding back, towards the hill with the little cabin that will be the only home I'll ever know. The one with a second room floor where I can fall apart without an audience.

But even that will have to wait, because first, I need to go after my heart. The one residing among strangers.

I remember the name of the town the merchant was headed for, so I know where I have to go. I may not be anything but an orphan in this world. But Finn and I can be orphans together. I can mother him like Ingerid did for me years ago.

The wind pierces through my clothes, and cold settles in my bones. But the freezing temperature has nothing on the ache that grinds its way into the depths of my soul.

If I made the right choice in turning away both Cian and Ask, then why does it hurt so badly?

CHAPTER 31

The wind snarling around the corners of the tavern fits my mood perfectly—I'd howl if I could, too. I'd let my pain rattle window panes, and screech my whimpers around the eaves.

But I'm not the wind, just a girl whose head aches from stifling her sobs to avoid disturbing the other travelers in the room.

I found a merchant to bring me south, but we're only one day's journey away from home, and the town I seek is another two if this storm keeps up.

In the darkness the hours left in the day, and my life, stretch before me like an endless road of loneliness and heartache. I wonder if Ingerid and Liisa realize what I've done by now. I let the serving girl at our tavern know, but who knows if she's had time to tell them yet.

When the proprietor's young wife comes down to stir the coals, I rise from the pallet on the floor. "Can I help you?"

She startles, but nods. "You can get this fire going so I can heat the porridge."

I kneel on the dirt floor and blow life into the embers. I

cough in the smoky air and pull in deep breaths away from the heat. Then I blow on the coals until a yellow flame bursts forth under my breath. The woman returns with a bucket of water, and together we make and serve up the meal. The merchant I convinced to take me along rises soon after, and I leave with him.

THE CREAK of leather harness and the horses' heavy snorts fill the air as the sleigh moves through the woods. Yellow sunshine bursts over snowy midwinter fields, and though it should make my heart feel light, it only reminds me of my grandmother's faerie stories.

We stop at a farm around midday, and the merchant ties up the horses to a fencepost and goes inside to barter with the farmer. I untie my scarves and hood and leave them on the sled. Then I walk through the powdery snow to stretch my legs after the hours cramped in the sleigh. When I circle back, I wipe the snow off the top rail of the fence and lean my forearms against it.

Movement in my peripheral vision turns my stomach cold with fear. But when I turn, my heart stops. The faerie I would rather forget—would do anything to forget, stands in the snow behind me. Tall, and familiar, and so handsome that I lose my tongue for a moment.

Were his eyes this green before?

"What are you doing here?" I gasp the words, as if I've forgotten to breathe since he arrived. And I might have.

He steps closer to me, and he's definitely never smelled this good. Like the coldest of midnights, fragrant spruce, and... cruel heartache. "I have a younger brother, other than Finn."

It's not at all what I expect him to say. "That's... nice." I lean against the fence for support as I wait for him to leave.

"He can rule Faerie as well as I can." Cian looks at me as if this is information I want. My heart smarts. Why would I care who rules Faerie?

"How fortunate." I turn around and brush more snow off the fence as if I'm on a mission to clear it off completely with my soggy mitten. "Why are you telling me? I'm just a stupid human."

"I'm telling *you*, Saoirse, because coming back here and seeing you wrapped around your safe choice made me realize that *a stupid human* is all I want." My heart quivers, and my lungs strain under the breath trapped there. "*This* stupid human."

He's so close to me his breath warms my bare neck, and gooseflesh springs forth over every inch of my skin. I will my body not to respond to him and force my stupid lungs to work. Cian doesn't get to show up here and take my breath away. Not after what he did.

That he can so easily forget the heartache he doled out doesn't mean I will. "And now you expect what? That I'll fall all over you?" My voice bites.

His chuckle does funny things to my legs, and suddenly they're boneless.

"I wouldn't complain if you did. But more than that..." His strong hands land on my upper arms, and he turns me gently towards him. "I need you to know that I'm sorry."

"No." I shake my head, and his face blurs. "Cian, I can't do this again. If you're looking for a temporary wife, please pick someone else."

I was a fool to say yes the first time. I don't regret it—can't regret giving Finn what little respite he's had for these last weeks, but Cian is no longer part of that. I'm going to find Finn and I won't rely on faerie or man to help me.

"I'm looking for one for eternity." His eyes don't leave mine. So green, so earnest that gazing into them hurts.

"I'm busy then." I drop my gaze to the snowy ground and swallow the sob that threatens to distort my voice. My tongue catches a salty tear at the corner of my mouth.

"How about till death do us part?" He drops down to one knee, and his eyes turn shiny. "Not for Finn this time, but for me?" Tears well in his eyes, and my own spill, too.

But his display of emotion changes nothing. I shake my head and try to dislodge the sob stuck in my throat. But instead, it escapes with my words. "You left me when you must have known what that would do to me. You knew everything I'd given up for you already, and you still left."

He shakes his head. "I was a coward, Saoirse. I thought I could give you up for my brother's sake, and I wish I could go back, but I can't." His voice breaks. "I have no right to ask for this, but please, can you find it in your heart to forgive me?"

His magic shimmers in the air around me, not touching, nor trying to overpower, just waiting for my answer.

I close my eyes, and he is everywhere.

But what can I tell him? The despair I've felt this last week has me worn and ragged. I don't want to feel this way anymore, would do anything to escape it. But forgive him? "I don't know if I can."

His head dips, and for a long moment, he doesn't speak. Then he exhales, and his shoulders slump—his eyes unreadable when they meet mine. "So this is it?"

Is it? The man I love, whose kisses make air feel excessive, is on his knees in front of me—asking me to choose him. *Not to rescue his brother this time, but him.*

And I'm about to turn him away. Forever.

He moves to get up, and before I have time to think, my hand shoots out to still him. He twists his head up, and his gaze moves to mine. "Saoirse?"

I open my mouth, but my voice doesn't carry, so I clear my throat and try again. "I need time, Cian. I can't just say I forgive you and move on."

Hope sparks in his darkened eyes. "I can give you time. What else do you need?"

I swallow. "I love you, and I want to be your wife…"

"But?" The knees of his breeches are darkened with moisture where they're planted in the snow, but he holds himself like a coiled spring, ready to launch into action at my words. If there's an action to be taken.

I swallow again and wet my lips. The temptation to shut him down is strong, but again, the memory of green eyes, too much like his, stop me. "You said it would be for you this time, but I'll only accept your proposal if it includes Finn."

The spark in his eyes fans into a flame even as his brows lower. "Which means?"

"I need you to give me time and reason to trust you. But before that, I want you to promise to do everything in your power to find Finn. And if he's unhappy where he is bring him home."

I don't say that I want him to live with us. I don't know if that's even possible. Finn deserves a way out of the hell he's been living regardless of who his salvation is. *But Saints, I hope it's me. I hope it's us.*

Cian swallows, still on his knees before me, his voice rough as he speaks. "I promise."

Relief rushes through me. I've asked him for time, and for help with Finn, and he's given both freely. I want to give him something, too. "Kissing Ask felt wrong."

Cian's face darkens, but his voice is exasperated, not angry. "I'm trying not to hate him, Saoirse. Bringing him up during my proposal isn't helping."

I huff out a laugh. "No, I just… I need you to know why I wanted him."

He rolls his eyes. "I *do* know why you wanted him—he's boring."

I shoot him a glance that makes him shut up. "I wanted him because I knew he'd keep me safe." I swallow and keep my eyes on my mittened hands. "My first memory is of watching the northern lights above my grandmother's cabin..."

I don't even need to close my eyes to see the iridescent bands of color uncoil in the dark skies, to feel the cold of that long ago winter against my cheeks. "And I thought that was magic. That the magical faeries she'd told me about fueled all I saw around me. The lights in the skies, the frigid snow, the sparkling icicles. All of it. And I..." My voice cracks.

Cian moves as if to stand, but I shake my head, and he stays where he is.

"I felt so protected, so cared for. Safe. And then, when she passed, I expected that magic to come for me."

"And it didn't." Cian's voice is filled with the same sadness that forged the chains around my heart.

"If it did, it brought me hell." I don't realize I'm crying until Cian is right there, smoothing my tears away with the rough pad of his thumb. He rests his forehead against mine.

"I wanted the magic to be real. In my mind it brought so much joy and beauty into my life. But then..." I swallow back my tears, but when I look at Cian, his eyes are so soft another tear slips out despite my efforts. I sniff. "After she died, it didn't matter anymore. The magic didn't keep me safe, and it still hurts, all these years later."

I try my best to calm my breathing, but it doesn't still the tears following in the tracks of the first. "But with you..." My voice cracks again, and I don't care that I must look ridiculous to him. "With you, I feel that magic again. And without that magic, the safety I felt with Ask wasn't what I thought it would be."

I reach out to run my fingers down his strong jaw. "I *need* safety, but I want…magic. I want you."

Cian clears his throat, his breath feathering over my face. "Safety is worth something, my heart, but you can ask for more than just that. You can have both—what you need *and* what you long for. And I can keep you safe. I promise you, I'll keep you safe, love. And Finn, too."

Safe isn't how I'd describe the way my heart thunders in my chest. And the world tilting as I gaze into Cian's eyes doesn't qualify either.

But then the faerie in front of me straightens to his full height, and his arms close around me. He holds me against his heart, and warmth spreads in my chest.

And for the first time in a long time, I dare pull in a deep breath.

Dare to hope that I'm truly that.

Safe.

⟳

CHAPTER 32

"You're still coming, girl?" The merchant steps up to untie his team of horses as Cian drops his arms and steps away from me.

I look around for Cian's horse. "How did you get here?"

He smirks at me, and I can't believe I asked.

"And can you take me with you that way?"

"Of course." He turns to the merchant. "I'll be bringing her to her destination."

The man frowns, then shrugs. "Suit yourselves."

I grab my bundle of clothes from the sleigh, fasten my hood and wrap my shawl around my neck. Then when the merchant and his team of horses are out of sight, Cian takes my hand and we walk into the woods. "How exactly are we doing this?"

Cian glances around at the snowladen trees and boulders surrounding us, then back at me. "I'll take you to the town where Finn is, and we'll find him and hear what he has to say."

I pull us to a halt. "How?"

A smile tugs at the corners of his mouth, and he lowers his voice. "Like this." He reaches his arms out, and I hesitate. I'm not ready to let him wrap me up in his arms as if nothing ever happened. Not yet.

He sighs, but doesn't let his arms fall to his sides. "It's the safest way to travel with two people, Saoirse, nothing else."

I step in between his arms and he wraps them around me. As soon as he does, the woods around us fade away into a blizzard. Strong winds tug at my clothes, whipping my skirts and threatening to pull me out of Cian's tight embrace. The noise is louder than cracking thunder, and I cling to him for dear life.

But right as I think I'm losing my grip on him, the sensation fades away, and the ground is firm under my feet again.

Cian lets go of me, but the world is still turning. As soon as I pull away, I lose the contents of my stomach in the snow. Cian's arm wraps around me, holding me up.

Once it's over, I reach for a fistful of snow to wipe my mouth.

"Are you alright, Saoirse?" He hasn't let go, but I can't even meet his eyes.

My voice sounds as weak as my legs feel. "I've felt better."

He snorts. "I dare say. Can you stand yet?" I push away from him, and surprisingly, stay upright. "Good. Now, are you ready to find Finn?"

"Yes."

I follow Cian through the silent, snowy woods. He holds the snowy branches out of my way, and I step directly into his cavernous boot prints to avoid snow melting into my stockings. It does anyways, and by the time we see the first houses of the town, my legs are numb.

The town looks much like the one I left, except that these buildings resemble Erkki's home more than our cabin. The house closest to us has windows with several green window panes fitted together. "Where is he, do you know?"

Cian frowns, but shakes his head. "I know the name of the

merchant that brought him here. Asking for him at the tavern is likely our best bet."

It takes us little time to locate the tavern, but when we walk inside the mood is quite different from the cheerful atmosphere of the one at home. The men seated inside watch us quietly over their jugs of ale, and their heavy gazes make my skin itch. I step closer to Cian, but their attention lingers.

Cian engages the girl stirring a pot of soup in the hearth. She listens to him with a bored expression. "Yeah, I saw the merchant with the boy."

I hold my breath as she continues. "His kin isn't around here anymore. The merchant left, but I don't know what he did with the boy."

My stomach goes cold. Finn isn't with his kin at all? Before she can go back to stirring, I speak up. "Where did the merchant go?"

She shrugs as if she has no interest in the answer, as if the fate of a child is no skin off her back. "Further south, I guess. He's not a regular in these parts."

Cian takes a quick look around the tavern, then grabs my hand and pulls me outside. I step away from him as soon as we're outside. "What are we going to do?"

His words are calm and collected, but his eyes look as worried as I feel. "We'll keep looking. We can follow the merchant as soon as we make sure he didn't leave Finn here."

I nod, trying not to choke with the fear snarling around my throat. Finn might be alone, and he's almost definitely scared. And I have no idea how to get him. Why did I let them take him away? Why didn't I try harder to get to keep him, or even to go with him?

I left him to fend for himself when I knew how uncertain his fate was. How am I any better than all the adults who failed me?

The snowy town spins around me, and I'm going to get sick.

Cian's hand is on my shoulder, but both his touch and his voice seem too far away. "Saoirse, I need you to breathe."

"I'm breathing." I huff.

He nods. "Yes, but slower, so you don't pass out."

I make an effort to breathe slowly in through my nose, and the village comes back into focus along with Cian's touch. I shrug out from under his hand. I need to think clearly if I'm going to find Finn, and Cian's touch has never made my thinking any clearer.

If Finn is here in town, where would he have gone?

Where would I have gone when I ran away from my aunt? I was older than him, but maybe it's not so different? "Let's walk around the back of the tavern to make sure he's not here."

Cian nods, and we turn the corner of the building and cross the short distance to the stables. Our steps in the filthy, hard-packed snow are unbearably quiet. My thoughts spin with possibilities, each one worse than the one before. "What do we do when we find him? You can't move us both like that, can you?"

He shakes his head. "No. We'll find a merchant going north."

I push out another breath, terrified of the panic crouching at the edges of my mind. I call out his name, hoping he's somewhere close by. "Finn?"

Inside the stables the air is warm and pungent with horse sweat and manure. My heart leaps as I see a boy of Finn's height and build leaning on a broom at the end of the aisle. But as he looks up, I see that he's older than Finn by several years.

When Cian asks him about whether or not he's seen Finn, he only shrugs. "I think he was here a few days ago. Don't remember if he kept going south or not."

I let out a growl of frustration, but Cian holds me back when I step forward to give the boy a piece of my mind. "Leave it, Saoirse. We'll find him."

"Probably should look better after your child, this isn't a

place for young ones." The young stablehand smirks and throws his broom into a corner. Cian turns me around and moves us towards the exit. But my heart feels as frozen as the darkening winter landscape around us.

I don't know what I'll do if we can't find him.

We walk down the road through town. Servants light torches, and the wavy glass panes of the tavern throw patches of light out onto the snow.

Soon it's dark. And Finn is still alone.

Cian's hand rubs my shoulder. "Where to next?"

I wrack my brain for where I'd go if I was alone and penniless again. Then I remember. "The smithy. I hid in the stables of one after I ran away from my aunt."

Cian rolls his eyes. "Is that why you have a soft spot for black smiths?" But I don't even dignify that with an answer.

It's a long trek before we get to the buildings of the smithy, placed far enough away from the rest of the town so flying sparks won't start a fire. The hollow clanging of iron striking iron makes me think of Ask.

How am I going to explain Cian's reentry into my life to him? But it doesn't matter. Not until we find Finn. *And we will find Finn.*

Cian grabs a torch, and I follow the snorts from a large draft horse to where he's stabled with four others. This stable is much nicer than the one at the tavern, and the air is sweet with the scent of fresh straw. I walk quickly down the swept aisle, peeking into every stall. I've already given up when I reach the last one.

In the half-dark, I almost don't spot the dark bundle in the corner, half covered up by yellow straw. A bundle that lets out a small snore.

My heart stills in my chest, and before I know what's happening, I'm kneeling on the straw beside it. "Finn?"

The bundle stirs, and the most beautiful face turns towards

me. A red line from the coat he used as a pillow marks his cheek, and he squints sleepily up at me. "Miss Saoirse?"

My heart melts and I can't speak. But I nod again and again, and his wobbly smile contorts as tears push past my lashes and down my cheeks.

He rubs his eyes with a dirty fist, but when I reach for him, he crawls into my arms. I don't know how long I sit there, rocking him in my arms. Then Cian touches my shoulder, and I look up at him.

No words come to my lips, but he nods. "I know." His eyes are red, too. "We should move to the tavern, find our way home."

I nod, and Finn crawls out of my lap.

"Where are you going?" Finn's voice is suddenly small and scared, as if we might have only come for a visit.

I pull him close again. "Home, and you're coming with us."

"My kin doesn't live here anymore." He sniffs. "And I'm hungry."

I nod, swiping at one more tear trailing down my cheek. "I know, love. Come, let's get you some food."

I look towards Cian. "Do you have coins?" I had only what I gave the merchant to take me down here, and it's long since gone.

"I have coins, love." His endearment sends a flutter across my skin.

"Enough for lodging tonight, too?"

He nods, and I turn to Finn, pulling off my mitten and tucking his cold hand into it. Then I wrap his other into my bare, warm one. His small hand curls into mine, and I have never felt so complete.

"You're really taking me home?" His voice is full of awe.

Cian falls into step beside us. "We're really taking you home."

By the time we make it back to the tavern, Finn can barely

stand. Cian hauls him up against his shoulder and carries him over the threshold, and my heart melts again.

Maybe my grandmother's tales were very wrong about faeries.

And maybe I was, too.

CHAPTER 33

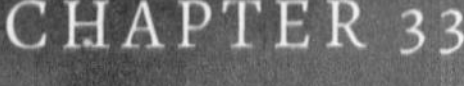

Cian carries Finn upstairs to the room he's secured for us, and my stomach fills with nerves. But he only tucks a snoring Finn under the woven blanket before turning to me. "I need to return to Faerie for the night. If you stay here with Finn, I'll come for you both in the morning."

I push out a breath. I'm spent after the day I've had—the swirling anxiety, the faerie travel, and trekking through the snow. "Do you have to go?"

"You don't want me to?" His green eyes are intent on mine.

I shake my head. "I don't want to be alone."

He glances towards the bed, where Finn turns over with a quiet grunt. "Come here." His voice is rougher than it was a minute ago as I slip into his outstretched arms. I rest my cheek against his warm chest and listen to the rhythmic beat of his heart.

I feel his lips against my hair, his breath hot against the top of my head. "You're not alone. I just need to return for a few hours. I'll be back long before you wake up. And I'll get you home, I promise."

I can't help the sob that slips out, or the silent shaking of my shoulders. This day has been all too much. This week. This life.

For several minutes, he rubs my back while I cry. When I'm able to talk again, I pull away. "I'm sorry."

He shakes his head and wipes the wet off my cheeks. "Don't be, love. You're exhausted. You need a good night's sleep, and you'll feel better." I nod and push out a weary breath, and he smiles. "I'll be back before you know it."

HE *IS* BACK before I know it. When I open my eyes it's to the red glow of the fatwood piece Cian is lighting, and I breathe out in relief. "You're back."

Finn stirs beside me as I sit up, and Cian glances at his brother with so much love it makes my heart hurt. "And I have a northgoing merchant ready to bring us home."

"Already?"

He smirks. "I found one last night before I left. He's going past your village, so we won't need to find anyone else."

I crawl out of bed and into his arms, and it feels a lot like coming home.

"I missed you." He murmurs the word against my hair, and I press closer.

Only the creak of the bed behind me makes me pull away. I turn and see Finn sitting up, looking disoriented and half-asleep. He squints. "Miss Saoirse?"

I sit back down on the bed and run my hand over his tousled hair. "Good morning, love. Did you sleep well?"

He nods and yawns. "Are we going home?"

I nod. "We're going home." I look at Cian, and then back to Finn. And the feeling pressing against my breastbone, so intense it hurts, is one I haven't felt in a long time—happiness.

We make it home hours after sunset, but Finn is still awake and talking up a storm. Cian leaves before we make it to the cabin with promises to be back by tomorrow.

As soon as I step inside, Ingerid throws herself around my neck. "Saoirse! How could you leave and not tell us? I've been so worried!"

I squeeze her tighter. "I know. I'm sorry. But I had to go and find him."

She drops her arms and looks beyond my shoulder. "Finn!" She hugs him just as tight, but he only looks shyly down at the floor as she leads him to the table and serves him up a bowlful of stew.

It smells heavenly, and my mouth waters. "Do you want a bowl, too?" Ingerid nods to me.

"Yes, please. I'm starving."

When Liisa returns home, her welcome is as heartfelt as Ingerid's, and by the time the house stills for the night, I let out a deep sigh of contentment.

Finn sleeps soundly on his bench, and I will not let anyone hurt him again.

I spend the next day baking honey cakes for Ingerid and Erkki's wedding feast. I feel a stab of guilt every time I see the evidence of wedding preparations I skipped out on by leaving town. But finding Finn was more important than all of it, and neither of the girls have said a word about it.

Liisa waltzes in the door just as I wrap the last honey cake.

The rosy glow of sunset gleams off her dark braids. Her cheeks are red, and her hood hangs uselessly down her back. She stomps her feet inside the door to dislodge the snow caked onto her skirts and stockings. She'll get sick if she keeps running about bareheaded like this.

I sigh. "Liisa, you need to keep your hood up. It's freezing out there!"

She startles and twists around so fast her twirling skirts spray snowy lumps in all directions. "What happened to you?" She shuts the door behind her, eyes still glued to my face. "Do you know how long it's been since you noticed anything around here?"

"No?"

She huffs. "I'm pretty sure I could have walked in here with a stab wound at any point in the last few weeks, and you wouldn't have noticed." Have I been that caught up in my fling with Cian?

She trails her eyes over my face again, then she gasps as her mouth forms a perfect "o." A knowing glint slides into her gaze. "Cian is back! He came back and begged for your forgiveness!" Of course her first guess is spot on.

I close my eyes, but the heat already rising in my cheeks betrays me, and Liisa's squeal reverberates through the room. "Saints! He did!"

I open my eyes to Liisa's victory dance. "Liisa! You're getting snow and water everywhere!"

But she only laughs. "I can't believe you forgave him!" Then she slaps a hand to her forehead and groans. "Ugh. I owe Erkki's friend a kiss now."

It's my turn to gasp. "Excuse me? You made a bet on our relationship?"

Liisa squirms a little. "Not exactly. He pestered me for one, and I thought if I told him he could kiss me if you and Cian made up, you'd be more likely to do so." She shrugs. "Unpleasant things seem to happen more easily than pleasant ones."

I roll my eyes and leave Liisa's ideas about the likelihood of misery alone for now. "Liisa, you know you don't have to kiss him if you don't want to, right? Regardless of what you promised?"

She rolls her eyes right back at me. "Maybe, but who's to stop him? He'll see the two of you around and know I'm holding out on him."

I don't know exactly how to get her out of this situation. But maybe getting my little sister out of scrapes isn't something I'll have to do alone anymore? "I'll have Cian talk to him."

"You'll what now?" The dark timbre of Cian's voice sets every nerve-ending alight, and I don't have to turn to know he's standing behind me. I turn anyways, of course, and my breath catches in my throat.

I saw him just hours ago, but it doesn't reduce the impact of him standing inside my cabin again. Especially now that I know he's in this for good… and that it might be safe for me to be so, too.

"She wants you to convince Erkki's friend that I don't owe him a kiss." Liisa says the words easily, but when I glance her way, her cheeks are rosier than before.

"I'd be happy to." Cian's gaze flits to Liisa only briefly, then it's right back on me.

"Right, I'll make myself scarce, then." Liisa shuffles past us, and soon the thump of her boots on the stairs reverberates through the cabin.

"Why are you here?" My gaze flits up to Cian's, but drops just as quickly. Having him in my space after pouring my heart out to him, makes me feel naked and vulnerable.

"You don't want me to be?" A frown mars that perfect forehead of his.

"It's not that, I just…" I swallow, because I do want him here.

He steps closer. "I thought we needed to talk."

My stomach sinks. "You changed your mind." *Don't trust the faeries.* I should have known it couldn't end like this. *My* story wouldn't. I shouldn't have—

His hand on my shoulder breaks the hold of my spiraling thoughts. He rolls his eyes. "I'm not changing my mind about you, but we need to talk about my keeping my promise."

It's my turn to frown. "Your… which one? You made several, as far as I remember."

"Finn. I got him home for you, but…." His words trail off as he pushes out a breath heavy with nerves. "If we are married…."

Hope smarts against my heart, jolting and uneven. "What do you mean *if* we're married?"

Shadows flicker over his face as he bores green eyes into me until I think he can see my very soul. "In this world our vows are sacred, but I wasn't sure if you still…."

He shrugs, and his wrinkled shirt tugs across his strong shoulders as he shoves his hands into the pockets of his breeches. "I'm a strange man in this town, with no family or connections. But now, with no kin to claim Finn, when it's us…" His words trail off, and the uncertainty in his eyes breaks my heart.

"He can stay with us?"

He dips his head, but wariness gleams in his eyes. He clears his throat. "I know you didn't ask me to move him in with us, but… I don't see how else I could do it."

I can't speak. My throat is thick, and the back of my eyes hurt. I push the words past the heart in my throat. "You think I'd refuse it?"

"It's not easy to take in a child his age. He's been through hell and back, and he'll have wounds that need healing. He'll likely be a difficult charge."

Suddenly, I can't stand the distance between us for another second. Can't bear the inches of smoky indoor air and flickering light. I step forward until Cian's solid chest is pressed to mine and slip my hands up to cup his perfect jaw. My thumb brushes across his full bottom lip only because I can't help it. He shivers under my touch and warmth spreads in my chest.

"Cian. I would be honored to share my home with you *and* your brother." I press a kiss to the side of his chin, and my neck breaks out in gooseflesh at the tremble that ripples through him. "Nothing could make me happier."

He swallows, and his eyes close as a whooshing breath leaves his chest. A tear catches the firelight as it pushes its way through his damp lashes, and his voice is gravelly. "Thank you."

I pull his face down to mine and press my forehead to his. When his eyes open, they have never been so green.

Never so bright.

Never so full of love.

"Saoirse…" His whisper, deep and raspy, heats the air between us. "You said you needed time. And I'll give it to you, all the time you need. But how long before you'll let me kiss you?"

Warmth spreads in my chest. "Are you asking if you can kiss me now?"

"I am."

I don't answer—too much happiness billows hot and bright in my chest. But I think the way my lips stretch in a smile so wide it hurts might clue him in.

And if that doesn't? Then, the press of my mouth to his.

Or maybe the way his chuckle reverberates between my lips.

Or the way he swallows my laugh.

And as his mouth learns mine again, the jagged, broken pieces of both our hearts melt a little more around the edges. Turn a little smoother—a little more healed.

A little closer to love, to life.

To home.

CHAPTER 34

I ngerid's honey-blonde hair cascades down the back of her blue wool dress, and the belt with Erkki's family silver is wrapped twice around her waist. Her wreath of dried flowers has her looking as beautiful as any faerie princess, and still none of her finery holds a candle to the joy on her face.

My heart aches as I watch her take her place at the altar of the old stave church, and I squeeze Cian's hand. "She's the most beautiful bride I've ever seen."

His breath warms my ear, sending sparks of pleasure down my spine. "You only say that because you didn't see mine." Happiness explodes in my chest, even though he's wrong.

I was a terrified bride who didn't even want to marry him. There's no way I looked anything like this. I've said yes to marry him again, but there is plenty of time to have an official wedding later, when we won't mess with Ingerid and Erkki's.

I roll my eyes at Cian, but I'm not about to engage in an argument that can only end with his hands around my waist and his mouth glued to mine. As much as I want that—*never stop wanting that,* I won't.

Not while the woven cord is being wrapped around my

sister and her husband's clasped hands. I hold my breath as they speak their sacred vows. *The same ones I spoke in the hollow with Cian—words that still weave our hearts together.*

Soon, the two of them walk down the aisle and out into the frozen night to the fiddler's somber tune. The church empties, and Cian, Finn, and I follow the crowd out into the cold.

The fiddler walks first, while the happy couple lead the long procession of guests behind him. Some hold torches aloft as they march through the snow to a much livelier tune. Once we reach Erkki's father's farm, the celebrations begin. Ingerid and Erkki are propped against the headboard in their bedroom, fully dressed and with the covers tucked up to their waists. A fiery blush burns in Ingerid's cheeks, and she laughs as Erkki whispers something in her ear. He stifles a yawn, but there will be no time for neither sleep nor anything else for hours yet.

The fiddler is perched at the end of their bed, and the party continues around the bride and groom as if they're not even there. Couples dance through the rooms, around the bed. Girls' dark skirts whirl, and colorful hair ribbons twirl through the air.

Men throw their coats to reveal bone-white linen shirts and fine suspenders. An older woman offers the newlyweds a plate of food as she passes through. The air brims with chatter and laughter, and since Erkki's father can afford it, the feast will keep going for the next three nights.

Finn squeezes my hand and runs off with two boys his age. A serving girl tops up my cup of ale, and I take a sip of the strong drink before offering it to Cian.

"Thank goodness our wedding wasn't like this." Cian shakes his head, and tips the cup up.

I bump him with my shoulder. "We didn't even have a wedding feast."

He sends me a wide-eyed look. "And this is what you want?"

From his aghast expression, I suspect faerie weddings are nothing like this.

I grimace. "Maybe not exactly this, but weddings have been this way for hundreds of years, and I don't think there's much chance it'll change before it's our turn."

When he looks at me this time, the heat in his eyes makes my stomach do a somersault. He grins, and I feel it all the way down to my toes. He bends to plant a kiss on my mouth. "How about I meet you outside?"

I push my way back through the crowd until I find Ingerid, still tucked into bed with her husband. She lights up when she sees me. "Please tell me you've come to keep us company!"

I shake my head. "Cian wants to go home."

She groans and sinks back against the headboard. "Of course, he does. And since he's not the groom tonight, he'll actually get to spend some time alone with you." She looks wistfully at Erkki, who tugs her close and plants a kiss on her cheek.

"I'm starting to think he made the better choice, marrying you in secret." Erkki winks at me, and I blush.

My gaze moves around the room, but no one seems to be listening to our conversation. "I'm sure we'll have to go through this eventually."

Erkki grins. "I will have absolutely no pity on him when that happens."

I laugh, kiss Ingerid goodbye, and weave through the crowd in search of my other sister. I find Liisa mid-dance with Erkki's friend, and she sends me a bashful smile as she waves me away.

Once I'm back outside, I'm distracted by a heated discussion by the stables. I can't make out any words, but Ask's face is red and Kari is moving her arms wildly, as if she's shooing away a goat. I hope Ask doesn't marry her—he deserves happiness, and the way she screeches at him now I don't think she'll bring him that.

I turn from the former lovers and find Cian behind me. With

a sigh of relief, I step into his arms. I still can't get over how much they feel like home. Tucked up against him, I pull in a deep breath of air saturated with spruce woods, and midnight, and... magic.

"You ready to go home?" His chuckle tips my heart upside down, and he bends to whisper in my ear. "Remember my ability to see desire? There was a moment earlier where I thought you were about to go up in flames."

I groan and hide my face in his neck, because though he's exaggerating, he's not wrong. So much for thinking I've been subtle.

Then I tug him towards the gate. "Let's find Finn and go home, then."

"I thought you'd never ask." He grins, and my heart is buoyant in my chest. But more than the buoyancy, is the way I feel when he wraps his arm around my shoulder and tugs me close to his warmth.

It feels like an old memory.

As if I'm back in the deep woods, watching coils of northern lights unfurl in the sky, tucked close to my grandmother's chest.

And again, the winter chill can bite all it wants, because next to me is safety and warmth—and home.

EPILOGUE

THE MAGICAL NORTHWOODS, ONE YEAR LATER

"**D**id you always believe in magic?" Finn is eleven now, and in the year he's stayed under my roof, he's gained both height and weight, and the ability to speak his mind.

Outside, the world is cold and dark, and the wind howls around the corners of our little cabin. But inside, flickering lamplight competes with the warmth of the crackling fire.

I push away from the doorway where I've watched Cian's strong hands wrestle another log into the iron stove. The flames lick over the dried wood, and light dances cheerily through the open grate as he shuts the door.

He stands and brushes the sawdust off his hands, only to leave powdered yellow patches on his dark breeches. My cheeks flush and it's not because of the heat from the stove. How does such an ordinary action make me wish that Finn's bedtime was much earlier? *Like right now.*

How can I spend all night next to this man and still long for just one more moment alone with him? I bite my lip, and meet Cian's green gaze.

He smirks, as if he knows exactly what I'm thinking. "It's been a long day, my love, hasn't it?"

I blush, and his grin widens.

I turn to the boy whose head reaches past my shoulder now and ruffle his wild, dark blonde hair. Finn is the spitting image of his brother. So much so that I sometimes wonder how I didn't see the likeness when I met them.

But then Finn was a very different child when he was only my neighbor. And the impish glint of mischief in eyes that look exactly like his brother's was rarely present then.

I run my fingers down his cheek, and shake my head. "No, I didn't always believe in magic. There were many years I didn't at all."

He gapes, and his gaze moves between me and the smirking faerie by the fire. "But… how could you not?"

How could I not? Finn would know better than anyone how I could not. His childhood after his parents died was fraught with angry outbursts and violence, much like mine after my grandmother passed. We were both children who were too busy trying to survive to have room for magic.

But though I'll tell him when he's older, Finn doesn't know my story yet, only his own.

"I *did* believe in magic when I was your age. My grandmother told me faerie stories from the day I was born. But when she died…" I pull in a deep breath. "I was more concerned about staying safe than believing in magic."

Cian tsks from the corner.

"She was plenty scared of the wicked faeries in those stories, though." His voice is grave, but he can't hide the laughter in his eyes, and my stomach flutters.

But Finn doesn't look at his brother—his troubled eyes are on me. "You're not going to die?"

My heart jolts at the uncertainty in his voice—bleeds at the knowledge of all the losses he's already suffered in his young life. "Oh, love, no." I wrap my arm around his shoulders, tug him close to me, and plant a kiss on his dark golden hair. "My grandmother was very old when she died."

He nods, and his shoulders lose some of their tension. I slip my hand into his and pull him over to the bench where we've spent so many evenings together listening to Cian's faerie stories. Stories that are both more beautiful and more terrifying than any my grandmother ever told.

"But Auntie Saoirse, how did you find *him* if you didn't believe in magic?" He points to his brother, the faerie who started all of this. The same one who's shot me heated looks all evening and does so even now.

I roll my eyes at Cian, tug Finn onto my lap, and wrap my arms around him. He barely fits there anymore, but he never protests. He's had too many years without mothering to complain now.

"Well, you see..." I meet my husband's glittering eyes across the room, and begin the story our boy has never heard, and that we will never tire from.

"I once was a girl who believed in magic..."

THE END

AUTHOR'S NOTE

AUTHOR'S NOTE

I was born and raised in Norway, but it's been many years since I've lived through the dark Nordic winters with its precious few hours of daylight, so I've tried to relay the experience to the best of my ability.

If you are a writer, and you are ever tempted to write an entire book basically set at night—there are probably many more profitable ways to give yourself a headache.

The fictional setting of the Northwoods is based on Finnskogen, an area in Norway named after its 17th century Finnish immigrants. Liisa and Erkki were given Finnish names to honor this link. Kari and Ingerid, and the Pedersens were given Norwegian names to honor my own heritage. Saoirse and Cian were given Irish names as a nod to my love and obsession with all things Ireland (and also because by the time I realized this story wasn't set in Ireland but in Scandinavia, it was much, much too late to change the main characters' names).

Saoirse's grandmother's stories were inspired by the Norwegian folklore that surrounded me as a child. That said, I've written this story with plenty of artistic license, and I can only hope that this has added to the story, not taken away from it.

TO MY READERS

As always, thank you for taking the time to read this little piece of my heart. And a special thanks to all of you who employed massive amounts of patience while waiting for me to finish writing this story that I honestly thought would be published a full eight months ago. Life (and death) got in the way, but it is finally here, and though it is a bit darker than my other stories, I truly hope you enjoyed it!

If you did (or honestly, if you just read it), please consider leaving a review on Amazon or Goodreads, so I can keep doing this writing thing.

Thank you!

ALSO BY AUSTIN RYAN

Tales From The Northwoods:

A Winter Proposal, A Nordic Folklore Fairy Tale Romance (Book 1)

A Traveller Bargain (Book 2) - Coming 2024

The Triangle of Spirits Series:

Pirate's Treasure, A Time Travel/Portal Fantasy Romance (Book 1)

Mermaid's Tale (Book 2) - Coming 2024

Stand Alones:

The Christmas Marriage Plot, A Norwegian Heritage Holiday
Romance

The Fairshaw Library, A Victorian Cozy Fantasy Romance

ACKNOWLEDGMENTS

On a September day in 2022, an author walked through a backyard in Pennsylvania, listening to a story about her friend's dark-striped tabby cat who spent his days traipsing the countryside, and his nights in the house—where he inevitably puked.

Said author suggested the tabby was really a faerie prince, tending to his kingdom by day, and staying at her friend's house at night, and that it was only the magical effort required to appear a cat for the whole night that made him puke.

Max, thank you for your contribution to this story, and cat-shifter romance as a genre. You are not forgotten.

Many thanks also to:

My Kieran—I will never understand what I did to get to love you. Your courage, kindness, and strength is on every page of this book.

My grandfather, Morfar—I think of you every time I sit down to write. Your pride in my books is my constant source of encouragement. Thank you for telling me your stories, last spring and this winter. Getting to sit by your bedside and hold your hand in those last days of your life, your broad shoulders weak with age and your grip still as strong, was an honor and a privilege. Thank you for staying until I made it home.

My grandmother, Mormor—It's just me and you now. Thank you for being my best friend, and for being the incredible real-life inspiration behind Saoirse's grandmother.

My favorite duck, Jenni Sauer—for your love, your friendship, and our hours of conversations (and scavenging). There's a million things I could write here, and none would ever come close to doing our friendship justice.

My world treasure, Tara Knott—for reading the entire book in three-chapter-chunks two days before I sent it to formatting, just to make sure it still made sense. I know you'll pretend it isn't true, but I could never do what I do without you. I love you always.

Lauren Wyant—for being my daily dose of sanity, and for always being down to brainstorm covers, and titles, and everything else. If I ever write a book about llama princesses, you know it will be dedicated to you.

My Virtual Roommate, Ingjerd Løvgren Auestad—for everything. Wait, is this a collective apartment now? IS IT A HOUSE?

My UnWriters not previously mentioned (Cat Wiant, Leeah Fisher, Jenny Baldwin, Vicky Esquivel, Kayleigh Wilkes, and Desarae Wisnoski)—for being in my corner. I have a shelf ready to fill with our books.

Maria Spada—for your magical cover design skills! I am blown away by your work!

My editor, Savanna Roberts—for believing in this book when I didn't, and for boosting my ego by laughing in all the right places. My books would exist only in watered-down versions with raging plot holes and ambiguous prose if not for your superior editing skills. Thank you!

My Beta Readers not previously mentioned (Jennie, Ashley, Anna Lisa, Anna Marie, Catie, Vi, Blake, Melody, Heather, Elisabeth, Melynne, and Shelby)—for taking time out of your busy schedules to read the early version of this story, and for all your encouraging feedback.

Marie, our imaginary kitchen maid—for always leaving me to clean up the kitchen. Actually, thanks for nothing, Marie.

ABOUT THE AUTHOR

AUSTIN RYAN was born and raised in Norway, and though she has ample experience with freezing winter woods and dark-striped tabby cats, not one of the latter has so far turned into a wickedly handsome faerie prince—much to her eternal disappointment.

She accidentally wrote a novel about a traumatized, broken-hearted girl who falls in love with a too handsome, too magical, faerie prince.

A Winter Proposal is her third full-length novel.

Austin lives with her family in Connecticut, surrounded by bookshelves, faerie lights, and freshly made bazzerals. When she is not editing for other authors, getting lost in their stories, or writing her own, you can find her on adventures with her favorite son—in the woods, by the ocean, and in the pages of books old and new.

You can connect with Austin at www.authoraustinryan.com, or on social media.

Facebook: AuthorAustinRyan
Instagram: AuthorAustinRyan
Goodreads: austinryan
Amazon: Austin Ryan